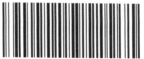

DAGGERS AND DAISIES

ARLIN CREED

This is a work of fiction. Names, characters, places, and incidents either are the product of the author's imagination or are used fictitiously. Any resemblance to actual persons, living or dead, events, or locales is entirely coincidental.

First paperback edition October 2022
Book design by Jennifer Curry/Canva
Map by Jennifer Curry/Inkarnate
Editor: Whitney Durapau
Playlist Organized by Whitney Durapau
ISBN: 9798218078089
Imprint: Chaotic Clockwork

Content Warning

This book contains depictions of sexually explicit scenes, sexual abuse; emotional, physical, and mental violence; and death. It contains mature language, themes, and content that may not be suitable for all readers. Reader discretion is advised.

Not every book is for every reader

To my inner circle:
my family, friends,
all those who believe in me.
And to every book that has ever ensconced me.

Mostly, to my husband, who when asked if he thought I could write a novel said, "You absolutely *can* write a book, but you won't."

Thank you for understanding how to properly motivate me.

When you create something new, you're breaking
tradition- which is an act of defiance.

-Steven Strogatz

Destrui: Earth Clan

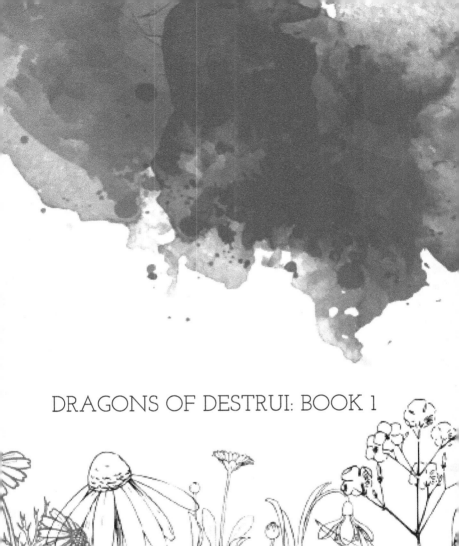

DRAGONS OF DESTRUI: BOOK 1

Table of Contents & Playlist

Prologue: The Master of Realms

The Clan's tiny hatchlings play outside my window, amusing me after a stressful day. Sitting back in my seat, I take a sip from the cold goblet clutched in my hand.

"Where is she?" I clear my throat, my voice harsh to my ears.

"Harvesting crops with the commoners," Hollis replies, a question in his voice.

"Digging in the gardens? Good," I muse, my mouth twitching up at the hatchlings taking flight before tackling each other in the field. Turning from my view I set my sights on Hollis.

"If I may ask, I've been with her for a long time. She's one of my best friends. I've never understood why someone of her stature digs around in the dirt, though," he shrugs before wringing his fingers together. His voice isn't judging, simply curious.

"Have you asked her?" I retort.

"She always replies that everyone who desires to eat should assist in producing it." He shrugs again, "I understand her meaning, but wondered if there was more to it. No one within her Royal Court would be caught dead doing the same. It's beneath them."

A scowl crosses my face unbidden. Staring into my drink observing the swirling amber liquid, I answer him with barely a rasp in the silent room,

"That's why they are dying. Scarlett is doing what she needs to do; what her soul calls for.

"I need you and Everett to remain with her. Don't leave her on her own. I listen to the Oracle, unlike the others. Her life will not be easy, I'm afraid, but she is destined for such great things." My lips twist in disgust as the words leave me, a pang shooting through my heart.

"She will be going through a transformation, all in the name of her realm. She is both their savior and their destroyer."

Hollis runs a hand through his hair while exhaling harshly, frustration clear in his eyes.

"She is the embodiment of good and evil; dark versus light. Scarlett is the goddess that they worship and the devil that they curse. In order for her to right what they have done to this land, she must first embrace the darkness that sleeps within her..."

My voice trails off, lowering, as I take in the fear expanding within Hollis's eyes.

Chapter 1

"Destrui is crumbling slowly."

The words come out soft, barely making a sound pass my lips. My heart breaks at the sight before me.

I stand looking out the window of my chambers, my long white hair being braided carefully around the crown of my head. The Earth Clan has always had an abundance of resources, but the once lush green fields are slowly turning to barren land. Scarred and bleeding soils patching their way in, drying rivers, trees shedding leaves dull and brown amongst their deep greens. Even the small farms and dwellings surrounding the outskirts of our clan are falling victim to the disease of our choices.

Sighing heavily, I wave my handmaid away from me, lift my skirts, and head toward the opposite side of my chamber where I can look upon the castle grounds. There is a bustle of mortals and creatures moving about, all preparing for the meeting of the Kings. The meeting where my ascendance is to be announced.

My handmaiden is busy fussing around me, trying to pin the drapes into place on my skirts, but I can't be bothered with such frivolousness; not when my whole world is about to change.

With a smile, I swat her hands, "Stop now, that is not necessary. They won't allow me to live long enough to care if my clothing is proper," I tease Malinda.

"Oh stop that, youngling. They will see you for what you are, and your father will stop at nothing to make them accept it," she reassures me, stabbing me sharply with a pin.

"Turn, missy, let me do your laces."

With arms spread wide, I give in to her demands.

"I'm a female, Mal. You know where that puts me," I whisper to her.

"Yes, a female, indeed, but a special one. You do not fit into the Clan. To any Clan. Surely, they will take this as a sign that it's time to reunite."

I glance into the looking glass, my white hair and pale skin clashing harshly against her brown hair and golden skin.

The laces pulling tight, I gulp air greedily.

"Besides," she whispers behind my back, "you are more than powerful enough. More than all of them, remember that."

I don't acknowledge her, just stare into the looking glass trying to see how my future will play out.

Seconds later, Malinda is pushing me out of the door. It creaks loudly behind me before closing. Pressing my hands into my belly and with one last deep breath, I make my way to the Council room. The worn stairs are layered in ornate gold and brown carpets, dulling the sound of my clunky heels. Rounding the stoned corner, whispers of the Royal Court make their way to me. The females and males scurry by quickly, not daring to make contact with the King's prized daughter.

The Council room is off to the side of the Throne Room, where the Kings and advisors of the Clans are meeting to discuss reuniting to save this realm. I stand patiently outside the door, awaiting my father's cue to enter. Each King representing the four elemental clans sit around the dark wooden table, with Father at the head. The sunlight streaming through the oval windows causes the room to sparkle in the early morning light.

"The entire realm is dying. If we don't do something soon, we will be gone before the next generation," I hear my father command the room.

"You can't seriously expect us to, what? Live together? Work together? That would be incomprehensible," King Ashur answers in return, twirling his Fire Clan ring around his smallest finger.

"Why not? Is your Clan too proud? Water dragons don't consider pride to be a humble trait," King Clayen refutes, laughter filling his voice. In his excitement, King Clayen knocks his goblet, the pale ale sloshing along the table. A handmaid rushes in, cleaning the spill quickly before running out to replenish his drink.

The males begin arguing amongst themselves, each one fighting to be heard over the other when an unexpected voice rings out over them.

"I have an idea." The voice halts, waiting for everyone's attention before continuing, "That should benefit us all," Alason states.

I didn't expect him to be back so soon and my heart rate kicks up at the sound of his voice.

I don't get to hear what his idea is before I'm ushered inside. My father is standing, hand held out toward me as I'm escorted by one of his advisors.

His voice rings out around the room, "This is my daughter, Scarlett."

All conversation halts at the sight of me interrupting their counsel. He continues, oblivious to the sneers being pointed in my direction. Kneeling at his feet, Father bows once to me before addressing the males.

"As I was saying, does anyone have suggestions on what is to be done?" Father begins again.

King Ashur flicks his wrist toward us, "It's well known that the different species don't coexist well. There are too many differences between us; it's caused fighting in the past."

There is a hum around the table in agreement.

"What about a hollow land?" King Larson begins. "Where could we meet to share resources? That way we're not directly putting the courts together."

"Not a bad idea, Lars-" Clayen begins.

"Not a bad idea? It's a terrible idea. Of course, the modest leader of the Winds would believe in sharing," King Ashur interjects.

Amusement fights its way onto my lips as the mighty males bicker amongst themselves.

Clearing his throat, Alason rises to his feet, refusing to make eye contact with Father as though he doesn't require anyone's approval. Regarding him with a sharp glare, Father cuts him off just as Alason opens his mouth.

"I've already been given the solution."

Alason scoffs, the voices of the Kings coming to a halt as they observe Father carefully. He holds out a hand to me, helping me to my feet. I keep my head high and chin up displaying grace and confidence.

"The next Queen of the Earth Clan, your Majesties, decreed by The Master himself."

My skin pebbles at the mention of this male, an icy breeze brushing soothingly over me.

The silence only lasts a moment before outrage erupts. Sexist slurs are thrown at me, some males get to their feet drawing swords and daggers from their belts. King Ashur from the Water Clan strides to the courtyard and shifts, flying away quickly, leaving his guard scurrying after him. My life is being threatened by the remaining males when my father raises his hand for silence.

"Now, I think it's time for peace among our creatures. That comes with change. I think that includes listening to the females among us."

His declaration is met with snarls and disgusted grunts.

I keep my position next to him, willing my face to stay a mask of calm. I won't bow to them, I won't let them know that they frighten me.

I was born for this role. I am the eldest child of the King, and they cannot deny me my birthright.

The gathering of males take their leave quickly, not bothering with the formalities of a proper council. I watch their flight, before finally turning to my father.

"That went well," I say sarcastically.

He nods, a happy smile crinkling his eyes, "It did. None of them tried to take a swing at you. That is the most important detail."

Rolling my eyes, I go to address his insanity when Alason's voice interrupts me.

"Father, Scarlett. I do have a solution for our Clan. For the entire realm. It could work."

I watch my father wave him off, taking up his seat again.

Alason sniffs loudly, rubbing his nose with the palm of his hand.

"Spring allergies, Alason? You should see the healer for that." His eyes crinkle as he smiles up at me. I stride over and throw my arms around him, squeezing tightly before falling into the seat next to him.

"What is this great idea, Alason? I didn't expect you to see you home so soon." I retort.

"You want to serve the Clan, yes?" I nod vigorously. "You could be useful. You're a special brand of difference. Destrui is dying because the gods are angry at us. You could help us rectify that situation."

I stare at him, considering his words. My eyes wander to Father, his face grim.

"Help how, Alason?" I ask.

"Well, you don't come from any of the Clans. Your complexion and coloring aren't congruent with Elementals. I've asked Father if you could have been from... higher up in the realm."

"What do you mean by higher up?" My lips purse as my eyebrows pull together.

"Among the clouds with the gods. Father, of course, dismissed the idea–"

"Alason, hold your tongue," my father grunts from the head of the table.

"Why should I? She wants to help, right?" he dismisses Father with a flick of his fingers, settling back on me, "Scarlett, you could be the savior of our world. You could be worshiped as a goddess in your own right. We just need a tiny favor."

"Who's we?" I ask at the same time my father spits,

"Alason, I told you no. It is out of the question."

"She should get to choose. If we could make the gods happy, they may forgive us our sins and heal our lands. Our Clan isn't the only one hurting. Water, Fire, Air– they may be stubborn, but they can't deny that they are fading away, as well. I need Scarlett to do her duty and be obedient."

"Obedient?" I parrot back to him.

"Yes, obedient. Do what you are told, no questions. That's what you females are taught, are you not? You do know how to follow directions, yes?"

I nod tightly, a sinking feeling erupting in my gut and sending chills racing down my arms.

"Good," Alason grins. "We're going to sacrifice you to the God of Aether."

"You'll do no such thing. I have orders that have to be followed," my father sneers at him, jumping to his feet.

"Order from who, Sire? Rules are meant to be broken, especially when we can save our lives," Alason retorts, rolling his eyes dramatically.

I blink rapidly at Alason, keeping my expression vacant,

"You wish to kill your Queen, Alason?" I ask, my voice even.

"Not *my* Queen, just sacrifice *you.* It's for the good of all. You need to think bigger than what is best for you. Don't be selfish." He sounds so sincere, I almost believe him.

"You'll do no such thing, Alason. Goddess help me, I'll sacrifice *you* to the Aether if you ever mention it again," my father growls.

I watch as Father struggles with his creature for a moment, his pupils transforming to a dragon's slits before returning to normal once more. Something I haven't witnessed since I was a hatchling.

Usually, he's much more in control of his emotions.

Without a word, I turn my back on both of them, stalking from the room. Alason calls my name, laughter at my expense filtering through. Refusing to acknowledge him, I step out onto the terrace and call my shift upon me.

As my bones bend and break, I take the shape of our true creatures, the dragons of legends. Launching myself into the sky, determination runs through my veins.

He can try to kill me all he wants, but I'll make sure I'm ready for him.

Circling the skies above the forest and mountains, I contemplate my plight. Seeking out the valley below, I aim and drop toward it. My claws scrape the soft ground as I slide to a stop.

Flowers are blooming fiercely, some taller than my beast. Except in one barren spot, the grass is low and tamed, with no plants spurting from the thick carpet.

Letting the change pass over, I examine the spot for a moment in my mortal form. Glancing at the forest lining the flat expanse, I check for onlookers.

Running the toe of my slippers back and forth across it, I close my eyes and send out my energy, searching. There is a stirring beneath the ground, its vibration calm and soothing. There is peace in this place.

I take a step back and open my eyes. Bending down to place my palm over the warm dense earth.

"Open to me, and me alone. For I seek the knowledge from the souls that roam."

The grass begins to recede into the earth. It reveals a small wooden door only big enough for one. Stooping down and prying it open, I take a deep breath and jump. Landing on the mud-made steps, I allow my eyes to adjust to my surroundings.

It is warm here, cozy even. Small candles are hooked onto the dirt walls. The bodies of those in Otherworld are trapped inside the Cists while their souls hover around the chamber protecting their knowledge from all who dare to enter.

Chapter 2

The library is dark and damp, the dim lighting causing me to squint. I take a deep breath, allowing the familiar musk to settle my rattled bones. Ignoring the black marble tombs that make up the dozens of Cists, I concentrate on my task. Running one finger along the rows of books, I search out the grimoire hiding amongst the mundane bound manuscripts.

The deep purple leather catches my attention. It appears almost black and unnoteworthy to the untrained eye, nothing stamped on the front or spine. As my finger comes into contact with it, an orb appears before me, glowing red with contained fire of indignation.

"Hush, now. I'm just coming to immerse myself. The knowledge that I seek I only wish for me," I whisper softly to the soul floating before me.

It whips away at my words, soaring into the rows of shelves around us.

Laughing softly at the fierceness in the soul, I carefully wedge the book out of its spot. Situating myself on the floor between two Cists, I close my eyes and let the spirits guide me to what I need.

To heal the world, I have to control the Elements. To live in this world, I cannot be finished before my time.

As the words float unbidden through my mind, the book flips open, pages turning quickly of their own accord. A violet smoke ripples out in small streams of mist, cocooning me in its secrets. I'm met with visions of a soul-cleansing ritual under the moon; a circle cast to open doors between worlds; an old male with blood dripping from his neck.

The images swirl quickly around me, moving faster than I can hold onto, allowing only a quick peek into each spell.

A floorboard creaks to my left and my head whips in the direction it emerged from. I slowly close the grimoire, trapping the mist and images safely back inside its pages. Placing it amongst the books on a lower shelf, I stand hunched and creep toward the intruder, keeping my back against the wooden shelves.

Slowly, I turn a corner and come face to face with a male. His golden blonde hair braided and hanging down his back. His eyes alight with humor, a crooked smile grazing his face.

My breath leaves me in a rush, my chest concaving on itself.

"Damn it, Hollis. You scared me," I laugh while pressing my hand to my chest to steady my racing heart.

"You're the one down here sneaking around with the dead. You've gotten absolutely filthy," he states, gesturing up and down my body.

"Did anyone follow you in?" I ask, standing on tiptoes, attempting to peer over his shoulder.

"And let them catch you playing with dark magic? Never," he grins down at me.

"I'm not playing with dark magic," I scoff back. "I'm just… learning. Knowledge is important, is it not?"

He laughs quietly as he runs his hands up and down my arms, warming them. His fingers linger on the cuts running from my elbow to my wrist.

"How did you get these?"

"That would be from helping the farmer today," I reply.

"I guess you didn't do a good job if he felt the need to attack you," Hollis quips.

"Not at all, he was very sweet. I fell trying to save his cabbage from the larkins."

He laughs loudly before tucking my hand into his elbow, shaking his head as he pats my hand into place.

"Only you. Well, that is a shame, and I feel as though you would be more... poised than to run around chasing furry little creatures," he teases.

I swat him in the chest playfully as he begins to lead me up the mud-carved stairs. We pause at the wooden door above our heads. Hollis holds up a finger to me in silence before lifting both arms and raising the platform an inch or two. Looking through the small gap, he nods once before shoving it open and climbing out.

Taking his proffered hand, I climb out slowly, looking around for those who could be spying. The valley is bright and sunny, not a soul hiding amongst the tall grasses or in the line of trees. The dull thud of the door falling back into place brings my attention back to Hollis as he stomps the patch of grass down over it again.

"Would you like to clean up before our meeting?" He asks, wiping the sweat from his face.

"No sense in cleaning up when you're just gonna throw me back in the dirt again," I laugh.

"I would never!" he mocks in a sham of outrage, throwing a splayed hand over his chest.

Shooting him a playful glare, I dust off my skirts and let him lead me through the trees.

Nearing the edge of the valley, I take off at a run. Hiking my skirts up around my thighs, I run and let the change overtake me. As I jump into the air, my body bending and breaking, my white dragon emerges. Circling in the sky twice before twisting and diving nose first into the lake.

When I resurface, Hollis is standing on the shore, amusement radiating from him.

"So, Scar, I guess we're practicing water today?" he asks.

My creature snorts at him before diving back under the water's surface. The cool water flows along my scales, a cleansing bath that restores and refreshes me after so long underground. A moment later I reemerge back into my mortal form, walking slowly back onto the lake's shore. In the palm of my hand, I hold a small drop of water allowing it to hover an inch above my skin.

"Impressive," Hollis grins, "but what else can you do?"

Grinning back at him, I stomp my foot and watch as the earth makes waves, gliding toward him before cresting and knocking his feet out from under him.

Splayed in the soft sand of the lake's shore he calls, "That's playing dirty, Scar. Don't you know you're supposed to tell your opponents what you're going to do before actually doing it?"

"No, I don't believe that's correct, Hollis. I think you just don't like me getting the upper hand on you," I smirk back, striding toward where he is lifting himself up to his elbows.

"I have nothing left to teach you, Scar," he mocks, hand on his chest and shaking his head sadly in defeat.

Laying down in the grass next to him, I close my eyes for a moment, letting the warm sun soak my face.

He hums softly at my answer, before changing the subject. "Want to tell me why you flew from the castle so quickly?"

"Not particularly. You'll go crazy if I do," I retort.

"Try me."

"Alason thinks sacrificing the 'freak' to Aether will buy us favor," I say lightly, hoping to diffuse his temper before it has a chance to take hold.

Hollis doesn't say anything but I can feel the tension radiating from him.

"I'll never understand the males of this Clan. Do they truly believe killing people will actually buy favor from the gods?" he muses, his voice low.

"Just the females," I murmur, "Apparently, that is my fate."

"*Apparently*, Alason just wants the throne for himself."

His words give me pause. *Maybe there could be more to his desire to see me beheaded.*

"When do you have to meet Consort Tilla?"

His abrupt change in conversation gives me whiplash. I take a deep breath, grateful to be done with this topic.

"Later. We are changing out the bedding in the chambers."

"I'll never understand why you feel the need to clean rooms when you have handmaids for that," he states dryly.

"That's because you've never had a hard day's work, Hollis. Honest work would cause you to keel over," I laugh.

He grabs at me, dragging me through the dirt toward him by my upper arm.

"Say what you want female, but I get enough work trying to keep you in my sights and out of trouble." He growls while digging his fingers in between my ribs.

I can't catch my breath as I laugh uncontrollably. Attempting to knock him off of me, I aim my fingers for his ears, pulling one hard before he moves to the tender flesh between my neck and shoulders, tickling me there and causing me to shriek.

Hunching forward, I attempt to push him over for leverage. He's not having any of it, pinning me down around my waist, he ups the stakes, digging harder into my flesh until laughter so loud rings out that tears begin to run down my face. Focusing on not letting my legs flail, I kick him solidly in the knee.

He finally relents and rolls off of me, laying in the grass next to the lake, both of us laughing as we catch our breath.

We fall silent, enjoying the warmth of each other's company. I close my eyes, giving myself to the warming of the sun.

"What were you doing in the Cists Library today?" he asks in between pants.

"Attempting to read the grimoire," I pant back.

He turns toward me, lying on his side, "Still trying to find a way out of your ascendance?" he asks quietly.

"No, just trying to learn everything I need to survive it. Nothing of interest today, just rituals and spellwork. Things that have been done in the past."

He nods, his eyes burning into the side of my face. When I don't offer anymore, he lies back down.

I absorb the moment letting it sick into my very soul, that calmness and serenity Hollis lends to me in my times of turmoil. Near him I'm able to forget the pressures of my expectations and duties, I can just be.

"Let me get you fed, then I need to leave for a while. Come on, we'll go into the village. I heard Tamer's Pub caught trought today."

"If I wanted trought, I could just shift and jump back into the lake. The beast is a great hunter," I shrug in response, not wanting this peace to end.

Tilting his head, he says, "I also heard that Tamer traded trought for some dekdra."

"Really?" I smirk. "I do love dekdra. Preferably with an ale."

I look toward Hollis, watching his smile grow along his profile.

"I think we could get some ale. Come on, up, let's go."

Letting Hollis pull me to my feet, I follow him back through the forest. Walking down the winding path in between the trees and shrubs, a thought occurs to me.

"Holl, where are you leaving to?"

He glances over, "I'm not *just* your guard, you know. I do have other responsibilities."

I nod sullenly, a feeling of remorse taking over the joy from our playing in the field.

"Of course." I pause for a moment, choosing my words carefully before asking, "Will you still be with me after my ascendance?"

"Of course, unless you don't want me that is," Hollis replies hesitantly pausing mid-stride.

"No, I do. I was just curious if this life was getting in the way of you and Oz."

"No. Oz is fine. She and Everett are going to be joining us at Tamer's."

"Really?" I ask.

"Why do you sound so surprised? I thought you and Oz got along. If you don't want her to come—"

"Not her. Everett. He doesn't usually choose to be in the company of others."

He shrugs, holding a branch out of the way for me.

"He loves you. Maybe he just wants to show support, *Your Highness.*"

"Dear goddess, don't call me that," I groan, rubbing my forehead with my fingertips.

He laughs loudly, threading my arm through his again and leads me onto the dirt street of the village.

Through the haze of the setting sun, I observe my surroundings. The commoners' huts are dark with dried clay, withering away with age. Pieces of the wire molding breaks through in large chunks, literally falling around those who live there. Not even large enough for anyone to shift within the privacy of their homes.

Only one more thing for me to make right for our people.

Shaking off the sullen mood, I look up at Hollis, watching him nod and smile at others as we pass. He loves all so equally and freely. He can make anyone feel at ease in his company causing everyone in our village to adore him.

The commoners stop us frequently, chatting about their day and showing me their wares for the market. I adore them, picking out something from each of them and handing over a penance. Hollis, ever indulgent to my whims, shoves everything in his pockets to hold.

The farmer from this morning comes bustling toward us, his silver hair pulled back into a bun off his face, his clothes hanging off him like rags.

"Dear Lottie! I got this for you," Saun yells as he runs toward us. Holding out a small silver container, he opens the lid. A white paste with flecks of green letting off the smell of eucalyptus rest inside.

"I felt so bad about your arm. Especially after all you do for me. Here, take this. It'll heal it right up."

Oh, this lovely male. This ointment from a healer would have cost him almost every coin he has.

"Saun!" I exclaim. "How lovely! Thank you, so much. Would you apply some on my arm for me? I'll only need a tiny bit."

I hold my arm out to him, keeping still while his shaky hands carefully apply the cream. Younglings run by, dust kicking up in their wake. Stopping in their games for only a moment to accept candies from Hollis's pockets.

Saun focuses hard, making sure to cover every bit evenly, struggling through the tremors wracking his body. His eyes come to mine, triumph and pride shining there, grinning like a youngling.

Examining the cut I gush, "This is magnificent! It feels so much better already, and look here, the swelling is already going down. You know, Saun, I'd feel terrible keeping all this for myself for just a few scratches. Take it home, please, use it however you like."

He nods fiercely, leaning in and kissing my forehead before shaking Hollis's hand.

"I've taken up enough of your time today, Lottie. I'll see you soon!"

A small smile graces my face as I watch him hobble away disappearing into the dust.

Chapter 3

As Hollis leads me toward the small pub, redirecting any more interruptions to our evening, I study the dirt beneath our feet.

We can't even afford a real road, indeed we could lay down cobblestone or something.

Hollis opens the door for me, the weathered, rotting wood squeaking loudly on its hinges. I step inside studying the dirt flooring, mud-caked and pitted, as always disgusted with the lack of care for our commoners. A sharp whistle from my right has my head snapping up, leaving my internal struggle behind. Hollis's hand lands on my back, directing me toward a small barrel in the back corner.

The tavern is busy this evening, mortals bustling about and laughing loudly in the dark dirty space. I wave and smile in greeting as we pass, most return it, but out of the corner of my eye, several point and whisper.

News about their Queen must be spreading. Feeling as though I'm on display, I consider running from the tavern to spare myself any potential hostility.

"I'm glad you saved us a table. Scarlett just *had* to take a swim before we came," I hear Hollis laugh from behind me.

My head jerks around and I come face to face with Everett and Oz. Oz is grinning at me, resting her head on her elbows while chewing on a flower stem. Her big brown eyes and tight brown curls are beautiful enough to make anyone, male or female, lust after her.

Everett is leaning back on his stool, a perky female standing next to him, rubbing his shoulder and batting her eyes at the mountain of a male. His sculpted arms are crossed over his chest, balancing on two of his stool's legs. He winks at the female before flicking his fingers and sending her away. Everett studies me quietly before nodding once and shifting his eyes to Hollis.

Taking my seat across the barrel from Everett, I watch Hollis lean down and kiss Oz briefly, my heart warming at the ridiculous grins they are both sporting.

"Scarlett, how goes it? I'm starving. I feel as though I've been here waiting for ages. Better now though, that you've brought Hollis back to me," Oz rambles.

I smile back at her, her rambling in reams defrosting the atmosphere brought on by my wayward thoughts. She's never one to hold her tongue, always so bright and cheery.

I smile back at her, "I'm well, Oz."

I turn my eyes to Everett.

"Everett, how are you? No, don't tell me. Let me guess, quiet and observant?" I tease him, sticking my tongue out before grinning.

He sticks his tongue in his cheek for a moment, tapping on the barrel between us with his long, thick fingers. His dark lashes narrow over light brown eyes. Muscles bulging against his brown and black Royal Guard uniform, the mountain-male motions me forward with two fingers. Leaning toward him on my elbows I study him carefully. He reaches out, running his fingers through the ends of my hair that escaped my braid. Wrapping thick strands around his fingers, he yanks down hard.

I swat his hand and pull back as he lets go.

"Everett!" I squeak. "I was just teasing you, there is no need for youngling games. Pulling hair should be beneath you."

He smirks at me, folding his arms over his chest and leaning back again.

Laughing softly I whisper loudly, "I love you too, Everett."

"Ale!" Hollis yells out from next to me.

A large clay pot is set on the barrel in front of us. Grinning, I look into the eyes of my friends just as Oz yells,

"Chug!"

Laughing, I take a dainty sip, while my eyes roam the room. Several females are waiting alone at different barrels, the hoods of their cloaks covering their faces. Lifting my chin towards one, I lean into my group of friends,

"They are here. Let's move this somewhere a little more private."

Oz nods quickly, getting up and swaggering over to a curtain-offed area with Hollis on her heels. One at a time, the females sitting alone get up to follow, each slipping behind the drape quickly and silently.

Sipping from the pot between me and Everett, I glance around quickly before we follow them.

The back room is dark and quiet as Everett and I enter. The females sitting cross-legged in the dirt with Oz heading the circle. Everett winks and blows air kisses to many of them before taking his position next to Hollis in the back.

"Here she is now, the Heir of our clan. Daughters of the Queen rejoice," Oz exclaims, grinning at me from her perch among the commoners.

I nod in acknowledgment before sitting down among them.

The excitement oozing from the females surrounding me is infectious, causing a buzz along my bones, lighting a fire within me.

"Drakainas, my ascendance has been announced. As you can imagine, the other clans didn't take it well. But, let's not fret, that's to be expected."

Ripples of exhilaration wind around the room as those among me break out in whispers and quiet gleeful laughter.

Oz clears her throat, effectively silencing the room again, "This has been a long time coming. We are all very excited about the changes a Queen will bring. We've discussed before the dreams we have. Let's stop dreaming and talk about what should happen. Who wants to start?"

Suggestions start flying around the room, each female demanding to be heard over the other.

"I'd like the option to choose whom I marry."

"What about *not* having to bare children?"

"Being allowed to leave our stations and marry."

"Getting rid of the dungeon fights to secure brides. It's barbaric."

I nod, praying that someone is taking notes. I take in their disheveled appearances as they talk amongst each other. Barefeet crusted with dirt and mud, some with open wounds oozing infection. Holes in their cloaks and skirts held together by sheer will.

Bodices that resemble nothing more than scraps of torn fabric. Faces gaunt with disease and hunger.

"Equal distribution." My voice rings out among the hushed tones of the others. Clearing my throat, I take a moment to look each mortal in the eye.

"Equal share of resources and food. Healing ourselves and the land has to come first. If we are strong and healthy, then we can deal with the laws of females."

I hold my breath as silence surrounds us, the females of my clan staring at me before glancing at each other uncertainly.

One brave soul poses the question that is burning in everyone's eyes, "Who cares about the land? There are more important issues to be dealt with."

Murmurs of agreement echo through the small space. Oz abandons her station, coming to sit beside me in the dirt with a look of sympathy.

I raise my hands in a request for silence,

"Everyone here should care about the land. It's dying. The Elemental Clans separating caused a rift to form, Our crops are withering before we can harvest and the game we have hunted for meat is almost extinct. Have you noticed it hasn't rained in a year? Or the grass dying beneath your feet? Hell, even our wells are drying up, soon there will be no water to drink. I've been told the other clans suffer the same fate, if not worse."

A warm hand encompasses mine, looking over a wrinkly face Malinda is grinning back at me. Borrowing her strength, I push on.

"It's Winter in the Fire Clan, a place that used to only have warm weather. The Air Clan has begun taking on water into their caves because it won't stop raining, flooding their homes and city."

I watch my words sink in, horror seeping into arrogant features. Rising to my feet, griping Oz and Malinda's hands, I end my tirade,

"This disease doesn't just affect the males in our world. It affects us and our children as well. The only goal here is to restore balance among us. Once we are able to have the land provide for us again then, and only then, can we break the Male Tradition."

I glance toward the dark back corner to see Hollis and Everett grinning and nodding their approval, eyes gleaming with pride.

Oz stands, holding her hands out above her, "Daughters of the Queen, all in favor say 'Aye'."

"That went well," I whisper to Hollis in the dark alley leading from the tavern.

He wraps an arm around my waist, pulling me into him causing us to stagger slightly before straightening again.

"It did. I applaud your insistence that to break from tradition, we have to heal our home first," Hollis whispers back.

"We do!" I insist, "Every time we meet with the female commoners, I get an overwhelming desire to wash and feed them."

Hollis holds me at arm's length and bends down so he's at my eye level, "You are quite literally, amazing."

"That's what you say to every First Queen," I retort, pointing at him and attempting to keep a straight face.

Hollis jerks me into him, tension coiling along his body. Confused at his sudden change in demeanor, I follow his line of sight.

On the road, directly in front of us, my mother stands. Hands clasped tightly in front of her with a disapproving frown upon her face.

I clear my throat, "Mother," I greet her.

"Scarlett. Females are not to roam at night," her stern voice rings out around us.

"Just trying to live a little, Mother. You know, before my responsibilities take over," I answer, dropping my sight to the dirt beneath my skirts.

Hollis releases me and takes a step back as Mother sighs deeply.

"Come with me, Scarlet, let's get you cleaned up and discuss your... whereabouts. We still have chores that aren't going to do themselves."

Swallowing thickly, I trail behind her. Keeping my footing steady and my head lowered. Ever the vision of submissiveness.

The water poured over my head in the tub is freezing. I squeeze my eyes shut and blow out slowly through my nose pretending not to be affected by the biting water. Mother sits on the stool next to me, watching as Mal begins to scrub at my scalp.

"The water would have been warm had you been back before the night was half over," Mother muses, her stare vacant.

"I'm disappointed in how you present yourself, Scarlett. Running around with the commoners."

"I know," I whisper back, keeping my gaze fixed on the stone wall across from me.

As Mal begins to scrub along my arms, Mother continues as though I've never spoken.

"You are to ascend. The first female in our realm's history. Do you know what this could mean? An actual Queen. Not as consort as I am, but someone with power. A female who could change the course of history for every female within our world. And yet, you waste it consorting with the commoners and trash. You keep hanging around them and you will become them, you know."

"Mother—" I try to interrupt the tirade.

"I'm serious, Scarlett. Spend time with the females of the court. They will assist you in learning your place. If the other clans find out about your group of 'uprisers' you could be accused of leading a revolt. Secret meetings in back-alley rooms full of filth. '*Daughters of the Queen*', indeed," she huffs, lips curling in disgust.

"As of now, females have no rights. You are to clean the home and breed. Nothing more. You are not even given a proper title, instead more closely regarded as a bastard of the King. You have the chance to change this, yet you kill me by trying to throw it away."

Having heard this lecture before, I tune her out. Closing my eyes and focusing on my breathing, I picture her suddenly becoming mute. The thought brings a smile to my lips, images of her mouth moving and moving but never a sound coming out.

A wack to my ear brings me back. Rubbing at the ringing brought on by the abuse, I bring my mother back into my focus.

"Lottie, I adore you, dear. I'm just trying to get you to stay focused." She says quietly, holding out a drying robe to me. Standing gingerly, Mal helps me out of the water.

Shrugging on the rove, Mother leads me to the stool she vacated. She waves Mal out and motions me toward the stool. Sitting down, I let her begin to comb my hair. In a soothing voice, she asks, "What are your plans, dear? What do you want for us?"

"To restore the balance, Mother," I tell her, my rehearsed answer spilling out effortlessly.

"Yes, yes I know that. That's all you ever say. Give me the real answer. The one that lies in your heart."

She kneels in front of me, tucking a wet piece of hair behind my ear. "No male will ever want to hear your mind, child. So, tell your mother. Only a female can understand such passions of the heart."

Focusing on a spot over her shoulder, I consider her words for a moment.

"I want a balanced world. One where the Clans can live together. One where a female's voice is as important and loud as a male's. Where the commoners are seen as equal to the royals. But even if that never happens, I just want to leave this realm better than I found it, where everyone is healthy and fed."

"Is that it?" She whispers.

I bring my gaze to hers, watching as a single tear tracks down her face.

"Isn't that enough?" I ask.

She nods her head quickly, "More than enough, Lottie. More than enough. And you, beautiful child, will achieve it. There is so much good in you," she places her hand over my heart, "right here. You love deeply. Even when they are not deserving."

I nod slowly, watching her face morph from concern to awe. Throwing my arms around her, I squeeze her to me, letting her soft flesh mold to mine.

"Tell me I can do this mother," I choke out into her hair.

"You can do anything, as soon as you're crowned. Just live long enough to achieve it."

I nod while pulling away from her. Standing and making my way toward my bed I pull on the dressing gown Malinda has laid out for me, laying the robe across the foot of the bed.

"Now, in an effort to get you to respect your station, you will accompany me and the females of the court in chores," she calls walking quickly from the room.

Following Mother out, I hiss quietly, "Why are *they* coming? It's always just us."

"You need training in your manners, child. Males like females who are submissive, quiet, and clean. You are *never* any of those things. I blame it on allowing you to roam the lands outside the palace." She shakes her head sadly, "I've failed in child rearing."

Rolling my eyes behind her, I curse under my breath while heading to the main floor.

On the other side of the castle, there are chambers for guests, far away from the family rooms to offer false security for those who stay. In a line outside the linen room, the females of the court stand at attention as they await directions for the guard. All dressed in heavy skirts and woolen cloaks. I stare at them as we approach, their faces downcast, desperately trying to make themselves fit into the boxes assigned by society. Mother greets them as I halt behind her.

"Drakanias. Scarlett is going to be assisting you in chores tonight."

As one, they lift their heads and look toward me, nodding their heads once before resuming their staring contest with the floor.

With mother leading the way, we march single-file, heading towards the guest chambers clutching silk-ivory linens to our chests.

The stone flooring is cool beneath my bare feet, grounding me in the present. I focus on the quiet echo of flesh against stone as we walk, ignoring the feeling of being in line to be slaughtered.

"Consort, Tilla! King Vika is requesting your presence," A guard calls loudly, tapping his staff against the floor in impatience. The other females flinch at the sound before resuming their work, each heading into the chamber Mother assigned them.

I watch as my mother's face falls for a moment before she turns to me.

"Take these cloths. Put them on the beds then go out and gather the wood. I have to meet with your father, I'll be back shortly."

She presses a finger to her temple, closing her eyes and focusing on the voice I know is speaking in her mind. Her face pinks slightly and she grins before looking at me again.

"Or maybe I won't be back. He's a rather thorough male."

She giggles quietly and makes her way back toward the family chambers.

Ugh, that's gross. Consorting with each other. Why would he have the guard announce that he's looking for her if he can just tell her through the mating bond?

I watch her disappear up the stairs, my smile fading. Wishing with my soul that I'll find a mate who creates such happiness for me. It causes an ache in my chest, a void that may never be filled.

I turn into the first chamber, that void making itself known.

"Why are you here?"

The soft voice startles me. Turning quickly, I set eyes on Lidia.

"Doing chores? Mother thinks I've forgotten my role as a female. I'm supposed to make friends with the court." I smile slightly at her slender face, steadying my racing heart.

"They don't want you here."

My head snaps back on my shoulders and my face must show my confusion because she pounces.

"You are a freak, *Queen Scarlett.* Your skin and hair are horrendous, you lack all the proprietary features that a female of our Clan should exhibit. The court hates you, don't try to be friends with anyone," Lidia rearranges the cloths she's holding before looking back at me.

I watch her, my eyes wide. My mouth opens and closes in succession, unsuccessful in attempting to get words out.

"I'm only telling you this as a friend. Stay away from the others. They support Alason's plan," her voice is soft and sweet, with not a hint of vengeance or anger.

I swallow thickly, tracking her movements as she leaves the chamber.

Good to know. Dismantling the court will be the first thing I do.

Chapter 4

Shaking off Lidia's ominous warning, I look around briefly at the rumpled sheets spilling from the bed to the floor.

Who slept here last? We haven't had company in days. Shaking my head, I begin stripping the sheets violently, letting my anger out. After I'm done refreshing the bed, I restack the fire, careful not to burn myself on the still glowing embers.

Maybe Alason is staying here. I don't know why he would be here instead of his chamber. Unless he's hosting company. Why is everyone around here suddenly coupling?

My lips pull up in disgust. Walking toward the bathing chamber, my eyes catch on a male in the sitting room off of the bedchamber. The door is only cracked, so I can just make out his dark brown hair. He's nodding at someone as he rises slowly and makes his way toward me.

Attempting to scuttle away, I trip over my dressing gown landing harshly on my side.

"My goddess. Are you alright?"

The voice is smooth and sweet like honey. Throwing the hair back from my face, I'm met with liquid green eyes cased in dark lashes. He's holding out a hand to me, on instinct I take it, dropping my head down toward my chest. My mother's voice plays out inside my mind. *Don't speak unless spoken to. Always appear demure and submissive.*

"I'm fine. Thank you. I didn't realize we had a current guest in this chamber," I whisper, dropping his hand and backing away quickly.

Turning and walking as fast as could be considered proper, his deep chuckle perplexes me.

"That was quite a warning from that other female."

I blanch, looking over my shoulder at him,

"You heard that?"

"Unfortunately," he says with a grimace, "It was brutal."

Remembering to practice my role, I bring my head back forward, eyes downcast as I make my way out.

"I'll see you around then?" he yells out from behind me.

I stop in my tracks just outside the door, my nature conflicting with manners.

My nature wins.

"Why do you think you'll see me around?" I ask turning back toward the male.

He's tall and gorgeous. Dark brown hair pushed back off his face. His strong jaw is only stubbled with hair, as though he forgot to shave.

"Let me rephrase, I hope to see you around." His eyes drop down my body before meeting my gaze again, a smirk on his full pink lips.

"I'm Maxim."

My manners kick back into gear and I tear my gaze away from his mouth. Curtsying, I reply, "Scarlett. Nice to meet you, Maxim."

"Scarlett." He rolls the sound around his lips, savoring it, "You are King Vika's daughter?"

I nod slowly.

"I am a very lucky male to be honored with your presence," the words purred out from deep in his throat.

I can't respond, all rational thought has left me at the sight of this male. His spoken words are causing heat to cover my face. I feel as though I'm panting, lusting over the sight of him.

He leans against the sitting room door, hands shoved into the pockets of his black trousers.

"Why are you in my chambers, Scarlett?"

My attention is on how tight he's pulling his trousers over his thighs. Heat and embarrassment fan my body, causing me to drop my eyes.

What the actual hell? Did I completely forget how to interact with the opposite sex?

"Chores," I manage to choke out.

"The type where you clean or the kind where you service?" The teasing suggestion in his voice causes panic to erupt in my chest.

I step back, eyes wide at what he is insinuating.

Without a response, I practically run all the way back to my chambers. My footsteps echo loudly through the empty halls. Throwing my room door open, I close it just as urgently and press my back against it. My breathing is loud in the quiet, placing a hand over my chest, I attempt to calm down.

For goddess sake, you'd think I've never seen an attractive male before.

Rolling my eyes at myself, still shaking with adrenaline, I climb into my bed and bury myself under the sheets. Visions of green eyes dance in my dreams.

Sitting in the brown fading grass under the tree, Hollis and Everett close by, I watch their interaction. Everett leaning against a wall while Hollis speaks quietly to him, retelling him of the Kings' meeting and

Alason's plan. Hollis is animated in his gestures, passionate about the story he is sharing. I smile at them briefly before despair settles in my gut.

"Don't fret so much, child. You're going to wrinkle your face if you keep frowning like that," Malinda scolds before rubbing her finger along the lines between my brows.

I grin at her for a moment, before grabbing her hand and tucking it into both of mine, "It's hard not to fret when I feel as though everyone is out to kill me.."

"Nonsense. I'm right here and I'm not out to kill you."

I laugh lightly, patting her hand before placing it back in her lap. Dragging my eyes away and taking in the members of the court milling around, my stomach drops as Lidia catches me staring. She looks away quickly, moving to stand behind her mate.

He roughly shoves something into her hands as he orders her away, pushing her roughly. Her face is passive as she falls to the ground. No one dares to intervene or help her, it is simply the way of things. Without complaint or embarrassment, Lidia picks herself up, eager to do his bidding.

This is the way I'm expected to behave, a slave to the males that hold power over me. Then after such rough treatment, I'm expected to bed them and bear their children.

I scowl, planning in my head how to rid our world of this plague.

It's not so common outside the court, some males even dote on their wives and mates, but most at least don't beat them.

Green eyes catch my attention. They are fixed solely on me, striding through the courtyard with purpose.

My heart rate kicks up at the sight of Maxim, the horror of running away from him last night deep in my bones.

I glance toward Hollis and Everett. They've noticed him approaching and are on alert. Quickly, I say a silent prayer that they won't embarrass me further.

"Scarlett. Lovely day."

He settles onto the grass next to me, watching Malinda over my shoulder for a moment before turning to me.

"I am so pleased to find you, I spent most of the night wandering the halls longing for you." His voice is low and inviting, daring me to lean in and taste his words.

Close enough to overhear Maxim's words, Hollis bears his teeth toward Maxim.

"Maxim. Lovely day," It comes out choked, a blush stealing across my face.

I am at a loss for words and immediately divert my eyes to the ground beneath us.

"I know we don't know each other well, but you are beautiful and fascinating. Would you be willing to take a walk with me? I have ideas of things we could get into," he waggles his brows at me.

Malinda begins coughing violently while trying to contain her laughter.

Gaping, I stare at him, not saying a word. Hollis is there seconds later, pulling him up by the neck of his cloak.

"What do you mean by coming here and attempting to proposition Scarlett? I could have you eaten for acting so brash, male," Hollis growls at him, wrapping a hand around the bottom of his jaw.

"Hollis put him down," Alason commands, coming up behind me.

Hollis doesn't even glance at him though, he is fixated purely on the male in his grasp. His claws are beginning to extend into the flesh of Maxim's face, blood trickling down his neck.

"Now, now," Alason chuckles. "Fighting and bloodshed may be the norm, but we don't treat our guests that way, Hollis."

I grab onto Malinda's sleeve, twisting it around my fingers as tension suffocates me. Everett walks up and places a hand on Hollis's shoulder, squeezing lightly.

Hollis throws Maxim to the ground, snarling in his face Hollis growls, "If I ever hear you insinuate *anything* improper toward Scarlett again, I will feed you to Everett."

Hollis stands, eyes locked on me, raging and full of anger. Turning on his heel, he stomps away, muttering curses to the realm. Everett smoothly steps in his place, taking over the leading of my guard.

Maxim picks himself up off the ground, straightening his brown-smocked shirt and running his hands through his hair as he looks around embarrassed.

Alason clasps him on the back roughly, before holding out a hand to me. Forcing myself to untie my fingers from Mal's dress, I accept it before rising to my feet as well.

"You should do something about that guard of yours, Scarlett," Alason scolds while assisting Maxim in correcting his cloak, wiping the dust from his shoulders.

"He wouldn't be a very good guard if he didn't defend me, now would he?" I retort, fighting the desire to snarl at the insult to Hollis.

Alason shakes his head in annoyance before addressing Maxim, "He can be a bit rough, nothing unusual about that around here though."

"I'm fine, perfectly fine," Maxim reassures him before turning to face me, the mask of charm firmly back in place, "I was just hoping for a meeting with the lovely Scarlett and I guess my wording was offensive in some way."

He's staring directly at me, eyes boring into mine with Alason positioned between us grinning broadly as he studies us. Warmth travels down my body, Maxim's unwavering attention is causing me to flush.

"Scarlett, why don't you and Max come inside? Father and Mother are waiting in the Council room for you. You can get to know each other a little better. I'm sensing chemistry between the two of you," Alason winks at Max, crooked teeth on full view.

Alason's observation embarrasses me, causing me to bite my lip and drop my gaze from the liquid fire burning in Max's eyes.

Max reaches out and tilts my head up with two fingers under my chin.

"Chemistry indeed," he whispers, winking at me as his gaze falls to my mouth.

Pulling my gaze away from him, I step out of his reach holding my hand out to Alason.

"Let's not keep Mother and Father waiting. Mal, I'll meet you later."

Alason glances at my outstretched hand before turning away quickly, his back to me as he hurriedly strides inside. Sensing my rejection, Max reaches out and intertwines our fingers, pulling me along. His hand feels like satin wrapping around mine. Planting my feet and stubbornly refusing to move, I tighten my hold and yank, fighting against his grip. Max turns to me, eyebrow lifted and staring me down with amusement before pointedly glancing around at those in the courtyard.

Pursing my lips and giving up the act of defiance so as not to draw attention from the court, I walk steadily with him. Making sure to keep my chin high. Malinda wiggles her fingers at me in farewell, hiding a grin behind her other hand.

The council room is brightly lit with torches along the walls, creating a semblance of cheer and celebration. Much different than the war room that it resembled yesterday.

"Ah! Finally! Scarlett, Maxim. Come and sit," My father calls, exuberant.

"Your Highness. Consort," Max greets bowing low before placing his hand on the small of my back and guiding me toward a chair at the table. Maxim's hand burns through the layers of my bodice, imprinting himself into my skin.

I wonder what his hand would feel like against my bare skin, no clothes in the way.

I clear my throat, sitting as Maxim pulls out my chair for me. Pleasantly surprised when he sits next to me, he pulls my hands from my lap and locks his fingers around mine.

I stare at them, the warmth they emit. His close presence causes bumps to pepper my skin. His thumb moves, rubbing up and down along the top of my hand. I'm mesmerized by the motion, my heart rate kicking up at the innocent contact.

"I'm glad that you are so taken with each other," Father smiles, pulling me from the fog that has overtaken my mind.

"Yes," Alason agrees, nodding, "when Max told me why he was traveling here, I knew."

Looking around the table, confusion marring my face.

"Knew what?"

"That the two of you would have a mate bond. I met Max while out training with the Guard. It seems as though he was traveling here following his bond.

"I spoke to Father about it last night after witnessing your interaction in Max's chamber. The court decided that you will be betrothed to Maxim."

Alason's smile drips in arrogance.

A moment later his words register, throwing Maxim's hand I stand, my chair falling backward with the violent motion.

"What do you mean betrothed? I am not to marry!"

Alason waves his hand at me in dismissal while Father rises to meet my stance.

"The King's Council decided it would be better if you were married, letting Maxim be crowned in your stead. A female being crowned is devastating. If Maxim marries you they will let him proceed as King since males are level-headed and not prone to fits of hysterics as the females are."

"I don't need a male, Father. I will be Queen. I intend to heal the land, reunite the clans, give laws to the females so they may live as the males. It was your idea, it's time we start listening to those we consider weaker."

He sits, crossing his hands in front of him on the table, "A consort behind a King is a much better position for you to make changes. It'll guarantee your safety."

My heart stops causing all time to stand still, blurring the edges of reality before pounding rapidly again. I can't hear anything over the beating filling my ears. Father's mouth is moving in slow motion as he gestures around the table but I can't make out a word. Dropping my head I stare at my hands, claws emerging from the tips of my fingers carving lines into the solid black wood as I pull them toward my body.

I jump when a hand is placed on my arm. Looking over my shoulder I see Max leaning forward, his face full of anger. Squeezing softly, he pushes to his feet,

"Your Highness, if I may. I have never intended to be crowned. Yes, the bond led me here, and the moment I laid my eyes upon Scarlett, I knew it was the gods' work. But I have no desire to be King of anything."

The passion playing through Max's words shocks me. His hand is closed tightly in a fist, pressed against his heart, eyes hard, and red in the face.

"I will marry my mate after she's been crowned. I will play consort to Her Majesty."

My father bangs his fist on the table, his temper taking control and causing my head to fly back toward him.

"You will die at the courts' hands." He looks toward my mother, studying her intensely before nodding once and continuing,

"Two days. You'll be crowned in two days. I hope you know what you're doing, Scarlett."

I out-stare him, determination singing through my body.

"I know exactly what I'm doing."

Max grabs my hand, pulling me toward him and forcing me out of the Council while I stare daggers into my family

Muttering under his breath in the dark corridor, he turns toward me, caging me against the wall.

"Do you wish to be Queen?" He asks, his voice low and menacing.

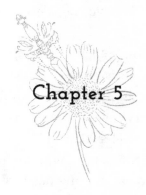

Chapter 5

Not daring to speak, I nod.

"Then let me woo you; let me court you. Let me show you that this bond is real. I feel it. You fell into my life last night, and I couldn't believe my luck. Since then, it's like a withering pain within me to be away from you."

He takes a deep breath, placing one hand on the wall on each side of my head.

"I stayed awake all night fighting the urge to go to you."

His eyes search mine, insatiable desire wafting off of him.

"Give me a chance. Please. I will make this work for us, My Queen."

I nod, letting his pleasure wash over me. Slowly and tenderly, Max kisses my forehead. My body heats, wishing for his lips to never leave my skin.

"You two should spend some time together," the moment shattered by Alason's booming voice.

Huffing loudly, I push Max away from me, crossing my arms over my chest.

"That's a great idea, Alason. Come on Lottie, it'll be fun," Max coaxes, reaching out and running his fingers along my cheek, soft as a feather.

"It's not proper. To be out alone with a male." I kick myself silently as the words leave my mouth.

Of all the times for my teachings to kick in, this is the one thing that I learned. Not to be alone with hot males? Ugh.

"You'll be in town, plenty around to witness what you're up to," Alason beams at us, wild and crazed.

Maxim cocks his head to the side, flipping his hair out of his eyes, "If we're already meant to be, then why fight it, love?"

This seems too good to be true, Maxim seems too good to be true. I'm only given one mate in this life, I should be honored he found his way to me.

Nodding once, I allow him to take my hand and lead me out of the hall and into the castle grounds.

"Just love me, Lottie, you know you want to," he grins at me.

He's cocky and ridiculous. Shaking my head, I look away from him before answering, "I don't know what you want from me Max, but I can guarantee you won't get it."

"I just want you to love me, let me guide and protect you."

"Guide and protect me," I snort, "I don't need guidance and protection from you," I smirk at him from below my lashes.

"How you wound me," Maxim deadpans.

Rolling my eyes at his theatrics, I look over my shoulder to see Alason waving us on, encouraging our time together. With a hand to the small of my back, Max leads me forward toward the small village outside the castle grounds.

I stop briefly, kneeling and smiling at a young hatchling attempting to make his dragon fly. I stroke softly along his tiny leathery wings, laughing loudly when he attempts to nip at my fingers.

"Playing with the commoners is really beneath you, Lottie. Maybe you should consider consorting with your own?" Max's voice causes me to rise promptly, glaring at him.

"My own doesn't accept me. In case you didn't notice last night, females don't hold positions here."

"Nonsense," he replies, waving off my words as he picks a flower from a bush.

"If they loved me, they would accept me into their court. Instead, I spend my time with the commoners, the farmers, and the creators. They don't treat me any differently because of what I look like. As opposed to the court who treats me as though I'm lesser than them."

He stares at me a moment, lips in a flat line, seemingly considering my words.

"You shouldn't discount your Queen's feelings or beliefs."

I turn sharply to see Oz standing behind me, eyes black as death as she stares into Maxim's soul.

Maxim is taken back for a moment, his eyes wide, "I'm sorry, who are you to be speaking to me in this way?" he stutters out.

"Best female to Scarlett. I would say friend, but my dear Hollis holds that place. You must be the idiot Hollis wants to take a bite out of. If Scarlett tells you how she feels about something, believe her. Don't wave her off. I've seen the court's treatment of her with my own eyes, they are cruel."

Her lips rise in distaste before she spits into the dirt between her and Maxim.

Regaining his composure and showing off his charm, Max straightens.

"Then they don't know what they are missing. You are far too kind and loving for anyone to doubt you, Lottie."

My heart warms at his words causing heat to cover my face.

"Are you hungry?" he asks, changing the topic.

"I could eat, I guess. Let's go to Tamers."

"Oh goodie. Hollis is there with Everett," Oz singsongs while rubbing her palms together.

Maxim glances at me before narrowing his eyes at Oz, "Who said you were invited?"

She scoffs roughly, looping her arm through mine, "I'm always invited. Isn't that right, Lottie?"

Trying to contain my grin, I nod once and let Oz lead me through the dirt of the village road.

Glancing back once, I watch Maxim drop the flower, destroying it as he digs it into the dirt with the heel of his boot.

Entering through the small door, I scan the room noticing Everett and Hollis at the back barrel. Hollis sees me a moment later, stiffening when he notices Maxim standing at my back. Oz takes off from me, rushing to Hollis and nuzzling him for a moment before settling herself in his lap.

Max pulls out a stool for me across from Everett. Sitting, I smooth my skirts, refusing to make eye contact with any of them.

Hollis breaks first, "Everett told me you all were in Council. What happened?" he speaks into Oz's hair, glaring over her head at Max.

"We are to be fasted," Maxim answers, his excitement spilling out. His smile is blindly beautiful and aimed directly at me.

"Of course, I'll never want to take her title so we'll wait until after her ascension."

"You sure about that? Not looking for a little power, *Max*?" Hollis spits back, golden eyes flashing.

"Of course not," Max scoffs. "I want nothing more than to be with my mate. And if being her consort means standing behind her and watching her rule, then so be it."

Everett falls off the stool he was leaning back on. The thud of his body hitting the dirt floor causes glances in our direction. Jumping off my stool, I race around the barrel, attempting to help him off the floor. Once he's on his feet again I make a fuss of dusting him off before he swats my hands away in irritation.

Hollis glances over at us, his knuckles white around the mug he's holding,

"My thoughts exactly, Ev."

His gaze bounces back to Max.

"Tell me, you blubbering idiot, why in the goddess do you believe you are Scarlett's mate?"

Oz is cooing into his ear, oblivious to the threats hanging in the air.

Max doesn't back down at the hostility being thrown at him. He stands, taking my hand in his before leading me back to my seat. Tucking a loose strand of hair behind my ear, he answers,

"Because a mating bond is sacred. It led me here to her. I can feel her emotions–I want to be her everything. The reason she smiles, her strength when she's weak, she's my reason for living and I hope that I'm hers."

I focus on his eyes, the sincerity in them causing my own to well up. I smile softly back at him. *He may be a blubbering idiot, but at least he's honest.*

"Is this male your mate, Scarlett? Say no and I'll end him here and now," Hollis growls.

What to say? Do I think he's my mate? No. Am I attracted to him? Hell yes.

"He says he is," I admit. "There is some... attraction there," I blush deeply, wishing the ground would open and swallow me.

"He is kinda hot," Oz interjects, finally pulling her lips from their worship of Hollis's neck.

Hollis glares at her for a moment, wrapping her long hair around his fist and tilting her head back before growling softly at her. Oz smirks and giggles in response. Hollis's hand sneaks lower, beneath view of the barrel's edge, causing Oz to let out a sharp squeak.

Hollis returns her smirk with a quick peck to her lips before letting her go and watching her walk toward the bar. He brings his gaze back to Max, watching him intently. The tension breaks as Everett clears his throat.

Holding up his mug in the gesture of a toast, he punches Hollis in the arm when he doesn't immediately comply. Grumbling, Hollis holds up his, as well.

"Since you're going to be around for a while, happy mating, I guess."

Leaving the tavern hours later, I watch the sky as we walk hand in hand in silence. Twinkling stars overhead creating the perfect backdrop for a romantic walk.

Is this really what a bond feels like? I imagined it much more magnetic and exciting. This falls flat in comparison to what I built up in my head. Let's not mention the fact that I'm being married to a male I just met.

My inner turmoil must be evident as we reach the iron gates to the castle's keep. Max pulls me into him, pressing my chest against his, his strong arms around my waist.

"I know that you are doubtful, love. How can you be sure of someone you've only just met? But I feel the bond strongly for you. Right now, you are questioning my every move. Wondering what it is I'm after. Let me calm your fears." He kisses the tip of my nose, a small smile lighting his face.

"You, just you is all I'm after. I knew the moment I found you sprawled on the floor of my chamber that it was you pulling me to this place." Breathing deeply, he closes his eyes, his face is the image of pure bliss.

"You have the most beautiful soul and mind. If you'd just accept the bond, you would know my intentions are true."

Bending down slightly in front of me, gaze locked on my lips, Max's tongue wets his own.

"I want to kiss you," he whispers, anxious with longing.

I freeze as panic sets in. Placing my hands on his chest I push him away.

If I kiss him would it cement the bond? I don't want to be beholden as Mother is, but his lips are so pink and full, though. I imagine that it would be the most decadent experience in the world. No. I need time to think about this.

"Give me time to adjust, Maxim. Besides, it's not proper to be running about kissing males."

Closing his eyes and exhaling heavily, he nods once before backing away, capturing my hands in his. Bowing low, he places a tender kiss on the back of my hand.

"Tomorrow then, little mate."

I watch as he slowly makes his way through the courtyard, hands stuffed into his pockets. Whistling a sad tune, Max disappears into the black of the night.

"He seems lovely."

I jump at the sound of Mal's voice. The smile I wear falls as I turn to her.

"Spying on me, Mal?" I question.

"Of course! You know, child, if I had a male like that hanging off my every word I'd never turn him down. How could you?"

"I may not..." I respond, trailing off and looking back to where he disappeared into the castle.

"You could do worse," she whispers, giddy.

Walking back into the castle with Malinda, Alason's voice booms out around me.

"How did it go?"

"There is no spark and he's an idiot," I lie, avoiding his gaze.

"Mating bonds take time, don't worry. You'll feel it soon," he assures me, rushing to walk along with us.

"No, I won't. He's stupid and trifling and very much below my status." I sniff, pointing my chin toward the ceiling.

He can't know that I like him, he'll start pushing Maxim to be crowned again.

"I do believe you protest too much," Alason teases before continuing, "Oh, think of the alliances you can make if you were to accept his proposal. The Clans will never accept you as a Queen, just as they do not see our mother as a Queen. She is nothing but a consort and you are nothing but the King's daughter. Father should have made me his next in line to the throne," he sighs dramatically, placing a hand on my shoulder.

"Alas, we all must face the consequences of that decision. If you want to rule and do so successfully, take my advice, Lottie. Give the male a chance, consider marriage, and submit to consort. You'll do much better as a consort behind her King than you ever will as a Queen that gets slaughtered on the first day."

Malinda's nails dig into the tender flesh of my arm, distress flowing through her.

Chapter 6

I consider what Alason said as I sit on my balcony. My decision weighs heavily on me. The choices are laid out before me and neither one appeals.

On one hand, I could be a consort behind the King; Making decisions and altering his ways to benefit our entire realm. Or I could give power to the females. I could stand and let my voice be heard. Look death in the face while I tear down every adversary. But what are the chances that I will succeed? Alason could be right and the Royals could slit my throat before the crown rests upon my head.

I crawl into bed my heart heavy with *what-ifs* and decisions I need to make quickly. I toss and turn before falling into a fitful sleep.

"Lottie we have company. Come, it's very important. Dress quickly." Mal is talking in hushed tones, bustling around the room.

"What has happened?" I ask, rubbing my eyes.

"Master Brenu is here. He is requesting an appearance."

"What does that have to do with me?" I force out around a yawn while lying back down and throwing the blankets over my head, snuggling back into my pillow.

"He would like to look upon you. Hurry now, we can't keep him waiting," she replies, ripping the sheets from me.

"It's the middle of the night, surely his appearance can wait until more appropriate hours," I moan, pushing strands of hair away from my mouth.

"He is The Master of Realms, Scarlett. We do not keep him waiting and he will not wait for anyone," she says rolling me toward the side of the bed. Her voice is panicky and rushed, her expression crazed with pins falling out of her hair.

I quickly dress, allowing Malinda to bustle my skirts and comb my hair.

"We don't have time to braid it. Here, pull it back behind your ears and bend. Your flower pins should work. There. Beautiful. Beautiful. Come now."

She rushes me out of the door, practically pushing me down the steps toward the Throne Room. Alason joins me in the hall, leading me down.

"Remember your place, Scarlett. Females are to be seen, not heard. Especially in front of The Master. Don't embarrass the Clan," Alason spits into my ear, leaving it cold and wet.

I nod, keeping my eyes down. Reaching the outside of the Throne Room, I take a deep breath and steady myself. Remembering to keep my eyes pointed towards the floor, so as to not offend, I follow behind Alason.

The stone floor is dull beneath me, showing paths taken by Royals over the years. Falling to my knees at the base of the Throne I keep my eyes downcast, waiting for Father to begin the meeting. There is a low rumble coming from where my father should be sitting, the sound comforting but concerning. I peek to the side, desperate to know why no one has spoken. Alason's face is drained of color, his mouth gaping like a fish.

He sputters, "What–you can't sit there. That is King Vika's throne. This is treason and blasphemy!"

"You would call treason on your Master?" The male on the throne exuberates command and obedience, his whiskey warm voice coating the room in ambiance. My stomach turns to knots, butterflies taking off in swarms, unable to break free from their cage.

"Young Alason, you have a lot to learn about respect. Perhaps you should kneel next to your sister, yes? It'll help you *remember your place*," The Master snipes, his tone bored and flat.

My lips attempt to pull up in a grin taking on a mind of their own, but I fight it off.

Alason getting chastised is worth being awoken in the middle of the night.

"Master, how lovely of you to make an appearance on this fine evening. How can we be of service to you?" Father sweeps in, his tone respectful and measured.

Father doesn't seem to have a problem with Master Brenu sitting on his throne.

"I only requested an appearance here tonight to share some wisdom and inspiration. But not with either of you." The air in the room comes to a halt, stifling and blistering around me.

"Beautiful Scarlett, it's such a shame to see you on your knees in such a manner. Stand."

I slowly lift my head looking towards Father and Alason, not daring myself to look upon this male.

"I did not command that you look at them, look at me," he growls.

My head snaps forward and I'm lost in the gorgeous male sitting before me, personifying peril and destruction. Beautiful and feral, to be awed and feared. Strong jaw under a full, thick beard; full lips that are pulled into a frown; his thick black hair is styled back, one curl falling into his face. He brushes it back before bringing his eyes to mine. I'm drawn to the intensity of his gaze, those butterflies in my stomach demanding I go to him. I pull back slightly in fear, *his eyes don't have any color.*

My attention is dragged away at the sight of Hollis and Everett standing at attention on each side of him. A grin on each of their faces, cocky and arrogant.

"Stand here. Let me look at you."

Gathering my skirts in my hand, I slowly approach the right side of the throne, drooping my sight on the intricate carpet beneath my feet.

"You two, you can leave. Take your guard with you. Allow us to converse privately," The Master demands, waving his fingers toward the hall.

Alason hedges, "It is improper for you to be left alone with a female of our Clan. Surely, Master, you understand this as you are the one who set the law."

"Do not put words in my mouth, Alason," The Master growls. "Those rules were put in place by mortals who do not understand the worthiness and sacredness of a female in the courts," his voice low and hard, his clear eyes blazing with flashes of gold streaking through.

"If you speak without permission again, you will regret it."

I watch as Alason sinks back, visibly shrinking in stature and looks at the ground before him. I try hard to hide my grin, desperately wanting to laugh at my brother's expense.

"Master, surely it would be wise to consult with the current leader of this Clan. I would be a better fit for any discussions of the future of our Mortals," my father pleads quietly.

"Get out."

The Master does not issue a demand, but a decree. His voice layering over itself, a slight echo ringing around us. The power in the words is a quiet promise of death, barely a whisper, daring to be ignored.

My Father bows low, "I didn't mean to disrespect my Master. Alason, come with me."

I watch as they both charge from the hall, their guard stalking behind them before returning to my observation of the male lounging across the throne, seemingly unaffected and without care.

It must be marvelous to have the type of presence that can send powerful males running from a room with their tails between their legs.

I bring my gaze over, watching Hollis and Everett for a moment, my eyes jumping back and forth. Hollis is sporting a small smile, one side of his mouth turned up in amusement while Everett winks at me.

"You do not fit in here, that is for a reason from the gods. You are the embodiment of everything pure that I created this realm to be. I would ask how you are fairing, but I can see for myself that you are not welcomed and respected by your peers. Add being a female to that, I imagine it is difficult for you," The Master muses softly, almost as though he's not talking to me, but rather voicing his thoughts out loud.

Some all-powerful male. Demands to speak to me and then rattles on about how hard my life must be.

Anger and annoyance fight within me, I attempt to keep it under wraps succeeding until his gaze locks with mine.

"What is that reason? If I am here to serve the will of the gods, to help heal the realm, why would they design me a female? Only a demon of a god would destine me to such suffering," I snap.

"A demon of a god, eh?"

"Well, maybe not a demon-god but definitely a brute. Could that be you, *Bru*tis?" I sneer.

Everett makes a slightly strained noise, my gaze flies to him as I watch him shake his head slightly.

My face pales, eyes wide. *I've offended him. My fucking mouth gets me in trouble every time.*

The Master narrows his eyes, tapping his finger against his bottom lip as he considers me.

"Don't call me Brutis. I don't care for it," he growls.

Properly chastised, I nod, letting my head fall forward.

That's what he's choosing to correct me on? Seems like only a slight compared to calling him a demon.

"I got a report that you tend to help the poor of your clan. Is that correct?"

Determined to be on my best behavior, I bow slightly before answering.

"Yes, Master."

"Why? I'm intrigued." He leans forward slightly, adjusting himself.

"Our lands need help, Master. They are dying and withering," I answer automatically.

"Look at me, I want to see your eyes when I speak with you, they are lovely." His voice is soft and warm, it could almost be called loving.

My head jerks up. I didn't realize I looked back toward the floor.

"You are very special, Scarlett. Hollis and Everett have told me great things."

"You know them?" I asked surprised, eyeballing them on each side of the throne.

"I know everyone," he grins, teasing me before sobering.

"How is this Maxim treating you?"

Woah. talk about a change in direction.

I'm taken aback for a moment, "Uh...Very well, thank you."

"Hmm. For his sake, let's pray he continues down the correct path. I hope you end up with a male who truly deserves and understands you. It would be a shame to have to endure someone who doesn't know what makes you... tick."

My mouth gapes open. *The nerve of him! I don't get a chance to respond my indignation. That is probably for the best, you undisciplined, drakaina.*

"I think I'll be back for your ascendance. This is a moment in history I don't want to miss. Until then, I'm leaving a guard with you."

He waves his hand toward the open courtyard as four males enter. Their cloaks are deep black with red stitching outlining their trousers and shirts.

"This is Abel, Xavier, Louie, and Alex. They are going to be... around," The Master introduces them.

"Tell no one that they are under my regime," he adds, but my focus is lost on the males. They each take turns nodding at the mention of their names. They are almost identical, standing along the wall with scowls on their faces, observing me. Only their hairstyles, beards, and tattoos make them distinguishable from one another.

I bring my gaze back to the male on the throne, a question brewing on the tip of my tongue.

He must read my mind because he continues, "They are to make sure that everything that is supposed to happen, does. Consider them your personal protection."

"From what, *Brutis*?" I ask irritation and confusion sweeping through me.

"From me, if you don't stop calling me that. I would have interesting ways of punishing you." He chuckles low, but it's not humorous. More deadly sounding than anything

"You're dismissed, E'tam," The Master murmurs, distracted, running a finger back and forth over his lower lip.

His gaze runs over me once, and I imagine a low purr sounding from his chest. I hesitate as feelings of guilt and torment wash over me, giving me an odd urge to comfort the demon-god sitting across from me. Shaking it off, I bow before turning my back on The Master of Realms.

Chapter 7

Leaving my room the next morning, I startle at the sight waiting to greet me in the hall. My eyebrows pull together as I take in the males standing at attention, in a two-by-two formation along the walls.

Pretend they don't exist and get on with your day.

Turning my back on them, I walk slowly down the stairs, stopping instantly at the sound of boots against the stone.

Are they following me?

My ears perk up as I continue down the stairs, the thudding of their boots following in my wake. I stop short again and so do they. Turning to face them, I find stoic expressions regarding me. Grimacing, I turn back toward the stairs, determined to find Hollis and have him send The Master's Guard away.

I trudge through the halls back and forth, calling his and Evererr's names and stopping handmaids in their duties to inquire after them, but I'm unable to find either anywhere within the castle.

I could make a game out of this.

Amusement fills me. I walk quickly and hear their pace increase. I walk slowly and they follow suit, slowing to a step once a minute. I stop and go frequently without warning, causing one to break and curse under his breath. I explore the castle thoroughly, making them follow me around aimlessly. I duck into the main library, scanning shelves and climbing ladders. I go through chores in all of the guest chambers, turning them into my little puppets and asking them to carry things for me.

Striding through the heavy front doors, a smile pursed on my lips, I wait patiently for someone to open the iron gates separating the royals from the commoners in the village.

"Scarlett!"

I turn toward the sound of Hollis's voice striding toward me. His lips are pulled into a thin line, but his eyes sparkle with amusement. Everett is next to him, a hand plastered over his mouth attempting to hide his grin.

"I've been looking everywhere for you, Holl! Can you please send these males away? They are in my way."

He looks over The Master's Guard for a moment before turning back to me.

"Is Abel carrying a set of sheets?" his voice trembles as he holds back a laugh.

Glancing back, I spot the disgruntled Abel with a bundle of white sheets tucked into his arms.

"Oh. I forgot about those. Whose bed didn't I make?" I ponder.

Everett's shoulders are shaking with silent laughter as he bites down on his fist.

"I can't send them away, Scar. In fact, you and I are overdue for our meeting and they are coming with us," Hollis tilts his head to the side toward the males.

My face falls, "Why would they come with us to the *meeting*? No one comes with us."

"Trust me, Scar, it'll be worth your time."

My gaze bounces between him and the Guard for a moment before I give in and sign, resigned.

"Let's go then."

Hollis laces my hand into his elbow and strides out the gate, The Master's Guard following behind.

Walking through the village quickly, the guard scaring off most of the commoners who would stop and speak with me. Disappearing into the edge of the forest, I make note of the direction we are heading.

"We're going back to the lake?" I turn over my shoulder, observing the males trudging behind us.

"As always."

We reach the clearing quickly and the males instantly fan out around me and Hollis in a circle, Everett joining them. I fault in my steps as I take in the hordes of females spanning the tree line of the field. The Daughters of the Queen, lounging in the shade near the lake's edge. I don't get a moment to comment on them being here when Hollis begins his meeting, gesturing to one of the males near me,

"You were introduced last night, but as a refresher–this is Abel." *Hair as black as night, cut short, almost to his scalp. Dark eyes that feel as though they could see through your soul. Towers over the rest. Scary as hell. Got it.*

Abel drops the sheets into the grass before flipping me off and grinning. His lack of beard makes him distinguishable amongst the group. I divert my gaze, focusing on the next male instead.

"Alex."

My, he is very handsome. And he knows it.

My cheeks heat as he waggles his brows at me.

"Xavier."

Xavier holds his arms out wide, turning in a circle before unfastening his cloak and pulling his shirt over his head. *Half of his torso is covered with a tattoo of a naked female. She's facing away from the audience, never revealing her face. It is a beautiful piece, sad and lonely.*

"Louie."

He's very childlike in appearance, with a face that is soft and trusting. Louie nods his head once showing respect that his counterparts lack.

My gaze tracks to Everett next. He's too busy glaring at Xavier's half-exposed body to notice my attention though.

"Master Brenu has explained to them that you are ... unique. I would like to go over what you can do. Louie here talked to Everett and came up with something they might be able to teach you," Hollis states, glaring at Xavier, as well.

My gaze bounces over to the females watching us with interest, Oz on her feet shielding her eyes with her hand to see better.

"Why would they need to teach me anything?" I ask distracted.

"Might save your life. The Master's plan was for you to be protected right? Consider this an extension of that."

I nod slowly, taking all of them in again. A vain attempt to commit their differences to memory.

"I want you to show them what you can already do."

"But, the females are here, and showing them and the Guard would mean—"

"Yes, your supporters should know how you will fight for them. It will be a good lesson to *all,* " his grin is devious, "I think you should start with Abel since he offered you such a vulgar gesture."

Unbothered, Abel swaggers toward us, his lips pulled up in that cocky half smile.

Turning my back on him, I address my audience, "My hands are unique. For instance, if I touch you with intent then that intent happens."

Turning back to Abel, I wiggle my fingers at him before pressing them against his shirt. A glowing white light appears, fanning out around my hand. I'm taken aback by the hues.

I trip over my words, amazed by his color, "Th- Th- This shows me the purity of his soul and intentions. The lighter the color, the purer the soul," I say quietly, almost to myself.

Shaking off the oddness of the moment, I push forward, "If I was to move my fingers like this, I could control his thoughts."

Abel's face becomes passive as I press them to his forehead.

"He's reliving his happiest memory. It also makes him open to suggestions such as: Abel, lie down and go to sleep."

Abel drops to the ground next to me, all control lost as his body collides into the grass with a dull thud.

Hollis beams with pride as he throws an arm over my shoulder, facing us toward the rest of the Guard.

Murmuring between the Daughters of the Queen breaks out, each one in astonishment.

"Impressive, obviously something you knew from birth—but are you any good with a weapon?"

Alex asks as he reaches into the back of his trousers, pulling out a dagger.

"Born with it?" I huff. "Some yes, but not all. I've studied and worked very hard to learn these things through the guidance of a grimoire."

"Okay. Got it, you have worked your ass off. But, if I were to run at you with this blade, what would you do?" he continues, turning it over between his palms.

"I don't subscribe to weapons. Females aren't allowed such things. I do keep a small blade under my skirts but, I have magic that most don't know about and of course, a dragon living within me," I reply, lifting an eyebrow at him.

He should know this. I just showed him. These males are slow.

"What would you do if you didn't have access to either of those things?" Alex's face is serious, contemplative.

He lunges forward, wrapping his arm around my neck, denying me the air I need to breathe.

"Pretend you don't have gifts. Pretend you are not a Destrui shifter. How could you get out of this?"

"Don't let her fingers touch you, Alex. She didn't tell you, but she could literally melt you," Hollis laughs from in front of us. He joins the other males, all standing wide-legged with smirks on their faces.

"Glad you all are entertained by the notion of me being attacked," I choke out.

Alex drops his arm, "Xavier, Louie, come assist."

They descend on me, rolling Abel's sleeping form out of the way, his arms and legs flopping at odd angles. Arranging my feet and arms in a battle stance they explain the different defensive maneuvers to me.

Once they have me where they want me, Xavier grabs my face,

"If I tried to kiss you, what would you do to fend me off?"

Eyes wide, I shake my head repeatedly, blurring his features.

"Go for his jewels, Scar," Hollis drawls out, amused.

"His *what?*"

Xavier's eyes glint dangerously as he lowers his face to mine, lips pursed and daring to get a breath away. Panicking, I try to scramble backward, but he follows.

Swallowing deeply, I bring my knee up aiming between his legs. Xavier catches the movement, stopping my knee just short of his crotch.

"Next time, don't panic. Louie, bring the knives."

Louie saunters over, holding out three different-sized daggers to me.

"We're going to give you a quick tutorial on how to use and hold these. Then we're going to show you where to hide them on your body. Usually on your thigh and ankle. Understand?"

My heart thumps loudly in my chest, sweat dripping down my bodice.

I think I understand the reasoning behind not letting females in the Guard. This is exhausting. Maybe if I had trousers like the males it would be easier.

I fall into the grass, closing my eyes and breathing deeply.

"Good job, Scar," Hollis beams at me before plopping down next to me.

Everett crouches down low, offering me a goblet of water. Taking it from him, I drink as though I'm dying.

"That was brutal," I gasp.

Everett nudges me on my knee, pointing over to Abel in the shade of the trees.

"Oh. We might need to wake him up soon. Think he'll be mad?"

"Abel? Of course, he will be. What are your plans for the rest of the day, Scar?"

"I think I'll roam over to Saun's, see if he needs help weeding or with the crops."

"Okay, Everett and I have to head back. We have a meeting we can't be late for and I want a chance to escort the females back into town, make sure they are safe. You'll be okay with the Guard?"

Looking over at the males hiding in the shade of the trees, I can't help but smirk,

"Yes, but could you ask them to not hover so much? As long as they can see me, they shouldn't have to be on top of me."

Hollis nods as he rises, helping Everett to his feet, as well. "As you wish."

I glance over at the Daughters of the Queen, all of them are on their feet talking and pointing excitedly toward me.

I hope I gave them something to believe in, things won't be this way forever. I'm sure of it.

Chapter 8

"Lottie. Lottie," Maxim's voice calls softly to me, floating from behind the trees in the forest. Looking around cautiously, I slow my movements. The Master's Guard stands at the edge of the road.

Glaring at me, I think. It's hard to tell since they are always scowling. They are just so merry and happy. The Merry Males.

Smirking at my private joke, I keep walking, making a loop through the forest around Maxim, getting closer to the large sycamore with each pass.

"Lottie, come here, Little Mate," Max sing-songs.

The smile in his voice causes me to smirk, holding back a giggle. His hand sneaks out, grabbing me around the waist, crushing me against his hardness. Our bodies flush, his masculine scent fills my nose as soft hands reach up and encase the sides of my face.

"I've been looking for you. I feel as though I can't breathe without you in my sight," he breathes out.

Max's eyes flame as he stares into mine, causing my breath to catch in my throat. I'm lost in the flames sweeping through his irises. My tongue sneaks out wetting my lower lip.

The movement causes him to fixate there, staring at my mouth.

"I've brought you something," he murmurs transfixed. He leans closer as though he's being physically pulled into me.

I look around quickly to make sure we are out of sight, "I deeply hope it's not what's beneath your trousers."

I try to tease him, instead, it comes out breathy and seductive instead of reprimanding.

A deep moan escapes his throat, the vibration from his chest causing a shiver to break out along my skin.

"No, that's for later, I think," he teases back.

Bending quickly, Max places a kiss between my eyes and backs away before I can protest the act of affection. Bending down he presents a bouquet of flowers.

"Daisies!" I gasp.

"I wanted to surprise you and something pulled me toward these. I hope you like them."

I finger the soft white petals, bringing them to my nose and breathing in their scent.

"They are my favorite. Thank you," I whisper to him, amazement flowing through me.

Mmm... must be the bond at work.

"Can I show you where I got them?"

There's so much hope and joy in Max's expression, I nod eagerly not wanting to crush his spirits.

"We have to fly, do you mind?

"Not at all, let me fetch..." I trail off, choosing my words carefully. "The Guards. Heightened security, you understand," I mutter remembering that I'm not to mention them to anyone.

He looks over my shoulder, his face falling. "I was hoping we could go alone."

I stare at him. "It isn't–"

"Proper. Yes, I know," he lets out a deep frustrated breath before continuing,

"Look, we're going to be fasted. We are mates. We deserve some time to ourselves without being hovered over. Don't you agree? Besides, don't you desire to break the rules sometimes?"

A grin works its way over my face.

"Thought so," Max picks me up, spinning me through the air.

"How do we get away from them though?" he asks, setting me down and pointing over my shoulder.

I gesture for him to follow me deeper into the woods, holding up a finger to be quiet.

Walking a short distance deeper into the trees, I take his hand in mine.

"Take a deep breath, Max."

As soon as the words leave my mouth, we dissipate. In a blink, we moved from the woods and landed next to a treehouse.

Looking around anxiously, he runs his hands up and down his arms, checking to see if he is still whole.

"We can fly from here," I grin at him.

Steadying himself, Max places a hand against his stomach.

"Teach me how to do that," Max demands.

My grin turns into a smile, beaming at him.

"Of course. Not right now though. You have something to show me, remember?"

He smiles back at me, stealing my breath with the beauty of it.

I set the flowers on the stairs leading up to the treehouse before lifting my face to the sky, and let the change wash over me.

My long neck swings around, Max still in his mortal form, his expression is one of awe.

"Beautiful, Lottie. Your creature is white." He approaches slowly, running his hand over the white scales along my side.

I nip playfully at his fingers and become mesmerized by his laugh. Stepping back and shifting, Max's large dragon appears. Hazel, a mix of green and brown. Curiosity overwhelms me as my head tilts to the side to study him.

Max nudges me with his head breaking my trance before returning the playful nip and taking off into the sky.

I leap up, following him. My wings beat the wind trying to catch up. Max turns, circling me in the air, hitting me once with his tail. A love tap, soft and gentle.

A sense of elation washes over my body, but it's not coming from me. Trying to focus on this foreign emotion, I watch as Max turns and dances in the sky for me.

He leads me toward a valley. From a distance, it appears to be covered in snow. Spiraling downward lazily, millions of daisies growing wild greet me, covering the earth like a thick blanket.

Touching down next to Max, I sniff them tenderly watching as they bend under the breath from my snout. They're tall, their stems thick, arching up and reaching to the under-blades of my wings, caressing the tender area.

A playful growl distracts me. Looking over, I see Max lowering his big scaled body down into the flowers. Only his eyes and the curve of his back visible in the ocean of flowers. His pupils turn to slits, his tail dragging lazily back and forth.

Oh, he wants to play.

My creature perks up, excited for a rump in the flowers.

Crouching down, I mimic his position.

He launches first, flipping me to my back, lightly digging his teeth into my neck, snorting. Using all my strength, I turn the tables on him, emerging as victor when I manage to pin him under me. He growls low and attempts to snap at my snout.

Daring to snuggle my head closer to his, I quickly lick the side of his face, watching as his body stills. Then again slowly as my body warms. Once again, that unfamiliar emotion washes over me: appreciation, warmth, lust. The breeze stops blowing, my oxygen drying up with it.

I back off of him quickly, scooting back onto my haunches, and let the shift bring me back to my mortal form. My breath is loud, chest heaving slightly as Max's creature watches me for a moment before doing the same.

On hands and knees, he crawls over to me. Planting his ass directly in front of where I'm resting on my knees.

"Do you feel it?" he asks quietly.

I shake my head, refusing to answer, to give credit to this insanity.

"These feelings you're having, they are normal," he whispers, grabbing my hands and running his thumbs along my palms.

"They don't feel like mine," I retort.

"That's because they aren't. They're mine. Well, most of them. I'm getting a hint of excitement from you. I don't know why the bond hasn't come to you yet…" he trails off staring at our clasped hands.

"Can I try something? Just a kiss. Please, I'm desperate," Max's words are choked, his emotion overwhelming him.

"I know it goes against everything, but we're getting married. It won't hurt anything," he continues.

His face is so full of hope and turmoil, the emotions he's emitting into me begging my soul to give in.

"Can I try something first?" I ask, staring at the oval buttons of his shirt.

He nods, a spark of joy floating to me.

I reach out to his chest and close my eyes, letting my fingers dig into the fabric of his shirt. His warmth seeps into me, running all the way up my arm. Concentrating, I let my energy wind out.

I watch as my hand glows with his intentions, a soft yellow. Pure soul and genuine intentions.

I pull my hand away when he grabs it, holding it against his heart.

"What did you just do?" he asks harshly, distrust painting onto his face.

His heart is pounding under my fingers.

"I tested your intentions, checked to see if you are pure."

His eyes light up, not as afraid as I expected him to be. The angry male vanishing in an instant.

"How did you learn that?" Excitement burns in his eyes.

I shrug. "I was born with it. I've taught myself to do all sorts of odd things," I reply, not yet trusting him with the knowledge of the grimoire or blessings from the gods.

"Can I see?" he rushes out, basically bouncing in his excitement.

I laugh softly, "No, but I can tell you that I carry the knowledge of souls and contain magic that isn't known to this realm. That's why Father chose me as heir."

And of course, Brutis forced him. But that's neither here nor there.

"Goddess, that's hot," he grins at me.

I roll my eyes, pulling my hand away from him, immediately missing his warmth.

Getting up on his knees, he crawls closer, invading my space and leaning into me.

"I let you try, now it's my turn," Max whispers, seduction lacing his voice. He grins, eyes gleaming in the low evening light.

Before I can protest, his hands are in my hair, and his lips are crashing against mine. A burning fire is taking over my body, adrenaline spikes through me causing my hands to shake.

Cautiously, I wrap my trembling hands around his biceps, amazed by the bulges hiding there. His tongue runs over my lips, causing me to hesitate for only a moment before opening to him. He moans loudly, pulling lightly on my braid and angling my head back.

He pushes us forward until I lay on my back among the overgrown flowers. My hands develop minds of their own as they run along his broad shoulders and down his back. He breaks from my mouth, moving his way around my face and down to my neck, kissing softly.

I'm too hot, my breathing too loud. This is amazing and I can't believe I made it to my maturity without ever experiencing a male's lips. I could die here in utter bliss.

His hands leave my hair, running up my sides, brushing lightly over the underside of my breasts. I startle at the contact, but he persists.

Fingers wander to the strings of my bodice, toying with them for only a moment before pulling them apart, exposing me.

I seize up, my hands falling to the ground frozen in fright and shock. Irritation washes over me, but it's not mine.

Max grinds out against the skin of my neck, "Don't stop."

I pull away, pushing him off of me as I sit up quickly.

"Do you know what the punishment is for a female in this position?" I hiss, attempting to close my bodice for a sense of modesty, "They could have me beheaded, you idiot."

"No one knows," he coos, inching back toward me, "Just you and me. Mating is to be expected, don't you think?"

His pupils are pinpricks, a greedy grin spreading over thin lips. His focus bounces between my lips and the hand holding my bodice up.

I want to push him away, tell him no. But the pounding in my chest matches the one below my skirts and it begs me not to.

Warring within myself, trying to decide right from wrong, Max decides for me.

Lips landing softly on mine, he coaxes me back down, slowly picking up where we left off.

My hands and lips become anxious as they come to life, pulling at his clothing and nipping at his mouth.

If I'm going to do this, I might as well enjoy it.

Rearing back, Max pulls off his cloak, tearing his shirt over his head. I'm met with the sight of dark hair spanning over his chest, fizzling out over his abs. Delicious muscles that I desperately want to taste.

Leaning down, he places his lips above the swell of my breast, pushing the bodice open again. My nipples pebble in the cooling evening air and Max licks his lips before capturing one and pulling hard. My back arches as a moan escapes me.

He continues to suck, alternating between the two as his hands creep down, bunching up my skirts with his fingers.

With the material lying at the top of my thighs, just short of exposing me, he sits back on his knees, eyes hooded, observing me.

"You're so fucking hot, little mate. How did I get so lucky?" reaching down, Max undoes the three buttons holding his trousers closed, reaches in, and pulls *it* out.

I avert my gaze, my cheeks heating. Max laughs lightly.

"You can look, little mate. Nothing to be embarrassed about."

"I've never done this before," I blurt out, slapping a hand over my mortified face.

Obviously, he fucking knows that, Scarlett.

Max chuckles, "I would hope not." His voice low and rumbling, filled with lust.

Slowly, I feel his body lay atop mine as he softly removes my hand from my face.

"Don't be shy, let me look at you."

He searches my face for a moment, love and lust battling within him, "I love you, Scarlett. You're the most amazing thing I could have ever been gifted with."

Pressing a soft kiss to my lips, emotion spills between us.

"And now, I'm going to make love to you."

He pushes slowly inside me, eyes not wavering from mine.

"Relax, Little, it won't hurt," he murmurs.

Taking a deep breath, I will myself to do as he's told. He rocks into me, slowly back and forth. It's uncomfortable and awkward.

What is he making that face for? Why does it feel like he's concentrating so hard?

"Close your eyes and feel, Little. Don't think so much," his hot breath coats my neck.

My eyes close, forcing myself to focus on the feel of him; on the in and out movement. The way he presses open-mouth kisses to my neck before nipping the tender flesh. The discomfort begins to slowly slip into pleasure, a growing ache I've never experienced. My body tightens, my muscles contracting.

Max groans against me, "That's better. Feel it and let go."

My fingers tangle in his hair, pulling his mouth against mine. My hips take on a life on their own, rotating in slow circles.

"Mmmm," he groans in appreciation.

A light, high-pitched sound bubbles up my throat. I clamp my lips shut and turn my head away, squeezing my eyes shut, my face hot in embarrassment.

"Goddess yes, let me hear you," Max growls.

My world is spinning as I try to register these new feelings, as I try to remember to just enjoy. Max bites hard into my shoulder and a fire-hot liquid runs through my veins. I wait for it to hurt, but instead, I groan in pleasure.

"More," I manage to say through my clenched teeth.

He obliges, sitting back on his knees and hammering into me. My body is spiraling upward, a wave of euphoria right out of reach. Max groans loudly, his movements chaotic before slumping over on top of me motionless.

He kisses my breast softly, laying on me sweating and breathing hard as minutes go by.

There is a tingling pain in my core that seems to be vanishing the longer we lay here.

"Gods, I love you, Scarlett," Max mumbles into my skin, "Did you finish?" he asks out of breath.

Reaching up, I scratch at my braid. "Umm, I don't know."

It comes out as a question, mortification wracking my body.

"You would know if you did. That's okay, though. Takes practice for the females, I've heard," Max chuckles.

Kissing me again, hard before lifting himself and tucking himself into his pants. I follow his lead, straightening my clothes and retying my bodice. Once he's dressed, Max fusses with my braid for a moment, securing it back in place and smoothing it down.

Something is leaking down my leg. I swallow harshly, attempting to use my skirts to dry the inside of my thighs without Max noticing.

"Let's get you home," he winks at me, shifting and soaring into the sky. I stand watching him fade into the horizon before begrudgingly following him.

Chapter 9

Dropping into the private courtyard of the castle, we shift back into our mortal skins.

Max kisses my fingers gently, "A very goodnight to you, Little Mate."

I watch him leave, warmth radiating through me. A smile permanently attached to my lips at his good mood.

Turning toward the stairs of my chamber, I bounce off a solid chest.

Reaching out to steady myself, I look up into the golden eyes of a very pissed-off Hollis.

"Where have you been?" he sneers quietly.

"Out," is all I reply, attempting to walk around him.

"The Guard has been searching the forest for you," he growls, following only steps behind me.

Reaching the landing, Everett is waiting outside my chambers leaning against the wall. He opens the door as I enter, following me and Hollis directly inside.

"I would ask where you've been, but you reek of sex," Hollis snarls at me, waving his hands through the air.

Rolling my eyes, I make my way toward the bathing chamber.

He follows me in, unperturbed.

"This isn't your concern, Hollis," I retort, my back to him as I focus on heating the water for the tub.

"I'm your Guard! It's my concern when you're potentially putting your life at risk!" Hollis yells.

Turning towards him, I smile at his bright red face. Everett leans against the doorway, watching us both with interest.

"Well, *Guard.* As you can see, I'm fine. No harm done. Why don't you put the Guard Sword away and be my friend for a bit? I need to discuss what's happening in my life."

Everett chuckles lightly as Hollis runs his hands through his hair.

"Fine," he bites out, "I'll let The Master's Guard know you are here. I'll be back with Oz in a bit."

The resignation in his voice causes me to laugh loudly, throwing myself into his arms and squeezing him to me.

He hugs me back quickly, before pushing me away.

"Seriously, you reek of fucking Max. Go take a bath," he laughs. "I'll leave Everett outside the door."

"Fucking, Max or *fucking* Max?" I quip

Leaning over, Hollis kisses my hair before shaking his head, muttering to himself as he leaves. Everett lingers a moment longer, lifting an eyebrow in question.

Smiling brightly at him, I wiggle my finger in his direction. He pushes himself off the frame, the door clicking shut behind him.

Toweling off my hair, I attempt to sniff at my skin to see if any trace of Max remains and I say a prayer that he's doing the same.

The quick knock at the door has me wandering out of the bath to witness Oz launching into the room, Hollis and Everett on her heels.

"Hollis told me you've been being bad, Lottie!" she squeals.

Flopping down onto my bed, I grab her, pulling her down with me, wrapping myself around her.

"I wasn't being *bad,* per se. Just exploring this mating bond that I was gifted with."

"Call it what you want, but you're supposed to be fasted first," she sing-songs.

"You are not married to Hollis, and you two do all sorts of *bad* things, Oz," I retort, narrowing my eyes at her. Hollis clears his throat loudly, faking a coughing spell.

"You have no proof of that, and neither does anyone else."

I roll my eyes, looking to where Hollis is situating himself against my headboard.

"You have ruined Oz and her standing Hollis, you should be ashamed," I chuckle.

"She started it," Hollis mumbles, staring at Oz adoringly before blowing her an air kiss.

Everett flops down across the end of the bed at my feet. Lying on his back, he puts one hand behind his head, the other resting on his belly.

"What do you think, Ev?"

Lifting the hand from his stomach, he waves it through the air in a so-so motion.

"Ugh. Of course, you take their side, you're a whore yourself. Stealing the virtue of every maiden you encounter."

Everett tuts at me while grinning as Hollis reprimands, "Language, Scar."

"Enough about us. We're dull. Tell me about Max. Was it nice? Did your bond click? How big is his—"

"Ozzie," Hollis growls as Everett laughs loudly.

I'm distracted from their bickering by the sound of Everett's laugh, rich and velvety.

I wish he would speak. He has such a beautiful sound to him, so deep that it feels like falling into a void. One where you would never want to escape from.

He catches me staring at him, winking before rolling over on his belly to face me. Following his motion, I lie down so that we are nose to nose.

Reaching out, he taps my nose softly, lifting that eyebrow again in question.

I shrug, thinking for a moment before answering him.

"I don't think I care for it."

Oz and Hollis stop whispering, their gazes heating the side of my face.

Everett motions for me to continue.

"It was awkward but nice. I don't think I did it right..." I trail off, not sure how to put it into words.

I watch as Everett's lip curls up, a look of disgust and disappointment filling his features.

"Hold up. Did he leave you hanging?" Oz whispers, outraged.

Still watching Everett, I nod sadly. Everett grunts before rolling his eyes.

"That's because he's a fucking idiot. It wasn't you, Max didn't do it right," Hollis growls out Everett's unspoken feelings.

"Want me to kill him?" Hollis asks, his voice full of hope and longing.

Laughter bubbles through me at his ridiculous suggestion. "No, that won't be necessary. I think it helped the bond. I can feel his emotions. And I ... I love him."

The room goes still at my words, everyone staring at me, their eyes wide.

Everett sits up as he shakes his head, clambering off the bed to lean against the opposite wall.

Oz runs a hand down my arm, "That's great, Scarlett. We're happy for you. It seems fast though." Her voice is soft and hesitant.

"That's how mating bonds work though, right? Love at first sight?" I ask, twisting my fingers into my sheets.

"We just worry. It seems odd to be happening now with your crowning," Hollis answers, unease filling the room.

Everett grunts in agreement.

How could they not be happy I found him? I was gifted my mate from the gods just as my life is going to get harder.

"Leave her be, Holly. Are you ready for tomorrow?" Oz asks, laying a hand on my arm.

Lifting my head I take a moment to stare at each of them, looking them in the eye.

"Yes." I project my confidence around the room letting them absorb the power that is being laid at my feet.

"We will be there with you. Every step of the way and if you perish, we will die along with you." Hollis's eyes burn into mine at his declaration.

Taking a deep breath, I let the possibility of my murder run through my mind.

I'll either die tomorrow or die for the favor of the gods. Either way, I won't remain in this realm.

Focusing on my fingers in my lap, my sorrow thickens the air.

"If everyone doesn't mind, I think I'd like to be alone now." Sadness pours through me drowning in a pool of my own fate.

"We didn't mean to upset you, Lottie," Oz whispers.

I don't answer her, just stare at the wall opposite instead. Hollis hugs me tightly as he gets off the bed following Oz from the room. Everett lingers for a moment, walking over to me and lifting my face toward his. Leaning down he places a kiss on my cheek. Placing a hand over my heart, pushing down twice.

"I love you too, Everett," I whisper, determined not to cry.

Lying in the silent darkness, I try to imagine what tomorrow will hold for me. I toss and turn, worrying over whether I will live to see the moon rise tomorrow. Images of destruction and death repeat in my mind. A never-ending flood of living nightmares.

Tapping at my door stirs me from my thoughts. Jolting up quickly, I'm greeted with the sight of Maxim peeking his head in.

He grins broadly at the sight of me.

"I was worried I would wake you."

"I can't seem to sleep. Why are you creeping around the castle at night? If anyone catches you in here..."

"Don't worry about that now. The entire castle sleeps, awaiting tomorrow's festivities," he whispers, crawling into the bed next to me. "I was lying awake, thinking about your lovely face, and felt the need to apologize."

"For what? You haven't done anything offensive to me."

"Oh, but I have. I believe I may have been... careless earlier this evening. I do believe I left you wanting in the daisies."

My cheeks heat and I break our eye contact. Not wanting to make him feel guilty or having any desire to relive that particular disappointment.

Disappointment indeed.

Tenderly, he bends down putting himself in my line of sight.

"I was so overcome with you earlier that I rushed. You'll have to let me make it up to you, little mate."

"How?"

"Like this," he whispers as he pulls the sheets from my naked body.

The next thing I know he's between my legs with his tongue licking up my center. I'm panting and pulling at his hair, finally falling over that crest.

What feels like hours later, Max is laying on top of me, sweat glistening down his back. Running my fingers along it, I smile.

"You're forgiven," I whisper into the darkness. Max chuckles sleepily.

"I would hope so. I think you broke me, Scarlett. I'm exhausted. Did I manage to help you forget about tomorrow, Little Mate?"

My body tenses at the mention of it, "Well, you *did.*"

He hums at my sarcasm before rolling over, tucking my head into his chest.

"I'll be right there with you, Little Mate."

The rhythm of his heart comforts me, empty promises securing me, as I finally drift into sleep.

Chapter 10

"You are going to miss your ascension!"

Eyes popping open, I pull the sheets off my face to see my mother standing near the open door tapping her foot, hand on her hips.

"Well don't just stare at me, get up," she insists.

I look toward the window, the moon welcoming me.

"Don't give me that face, you have no idea what needs to be done before the high sun. Oh, and The Master is already here, agitating your father and brother to no end."

Pulling back the sheets, I remember that Max was here when I fell asleep. Panic setting in, I let my gaze wander, but I don't see any hint of him. My eyes settle on Mal in the bathing chamber, holding a finger to her lips.

Wrapping the sheet around my naked form I look at my mother.

"I know there is plenty to do. After today I will have immense responsibility. I'm asking that you give me time to bathe alone while I meditate and ask the gods for favor."

Her face goes ashen at my words.

"Oh dear, I didn't realize that you were taking this so seriously. Yes, I'll wait out in the hall. Malinda will be in when you are ready."

I watch her go, keeping my face serious to match my words. Once the door clicks closed, Malinda runs out gathering up the sheets from my bed, stuffing them inside the bottom drawer of my chest.

"Have you lost your mind, child? You're lucky it was me that found you coupled up, naked with a male," she scolds quietly.

Running into the bathing room, I draw the water as hot as I can.

Mal shuffles in after me, "Not to worry, I sent him on his way. He is quite the specimen. Still, I worry over that arrogance he has."

Settling into the tub, I scrub every part of me that Max touched.

"Thank you, Mal. In a few hours, it won't matter that I've mated outside of marriage," I whisper back, running the soap through my hair.

"Yes. I know. But right now it could end you. I did not spend all these years raising you up to watch everything you desire be taken away because of a careless decision. If that male loved you, he would have seen that, too. I do understand the temptation, though."

She roughly runs a comb through my wet locks before hauling me out of the tub and toweling me off. Grabbing her shoulders to still her frantic movements, I place a kiss on her lips,

"I love you, Mal. Thank you for fixing my fuck-ups all these years."

"Watch your language, child. Now, I have to go find somewhere to be so your Mother can stumble across me. I'll burn those sheets later."

I grin after her as she rushes to the door and sneaks out.

Dressing in a bathing gown, I walk around the room lighting incense, one for each elemental of our realm. Finding my calm and centering myself I cast a circle on the floor in front of my windows. Sitting the incense down next to me before kneeling and bowing my head.

I attempt to clear my mind, connecting with the soul of the realm, seeking out the gods for guidance.

Purple mist rises from my upturned palms, winding in a river of smoke. I'm lost to the messages of the gods. They are speaking through me, conveying images. I'm met with visions of death and destruction.

I don't realize I'm chanting until a hand lands on my shoulder. It doesn't break the connection, instead intensifying it. The visions become clearer, the words pouring from my lips.

"Live and die. You'll remain on this site. Live and die, remain on this site."

The Master of Realms appears before me and it takes a moment before I realize it's not a vision. He's sitting cross-legged in the circle with me.

Blinking rapidly, I look at where his hand lies on my shoulder. His palm burns hot through my bathing gown, a tingling residing under it.

He removes his hand quickly, placing it on his lap.

"Did you know that your eyes glow when you connect with the gods?" he muses quietly, his eyes roaming over my form.

"You've been here quite a while, Scarlett. I've sent everyone away. Care to share what you've learned on your journey?"

I swallow thickly, noting the rising sun behind him.

"The future is bleak, Master."

My voice comes out with a rasp. I rub at my sore throat before stretching and flexing my muscles against the strain of not moving for so long.

"Who taught you to cast?" he asks quietly.

I shrug, "Just something I've always known. I have... gifts."

"Yes, I know, this particular one just surprised me."

"Why are you here, Master?"

"I need to prepare you for the ceremony. I've only ever passed my knowledge on to the first King. But as the first female, I felt you deserved my full attention, something a bit more special."

"Would you like to move to the sitting room?" I ask, remembering that we are sitting on the hard wooden floor.

"No, actually I prefer the casting circle. Seems appropriate for the ritual."

I watch him remove a match, a half-circle needle, and thread from his pocket.

"As a leader, we must be strong and fair," Master begins, "Turn around, Scarlett."

He reaches up to my shoulders, sliding my bathing robe down my arms and back. The movement soft and caressing, one finger sliding down my spine and lingering there.

"Cover yourself, I just need access to your back," his voice is deep, solemn as it washes over me.

Looking over my shoulder with the silk pressed against my breasts, he holds the thread up for me to examine.

Midnight blue and glittering.

"This represents a connection to me and our realm. The art of sewing tattoos is lost to mortals, they use ink now. But this one is special."

His brow knits together as he focuses on threading the needle.

"Relight your incense, Scarlett."

I do as he bids me, not bothering to get up. I will my energy out and watch as each stick lights and begins to burn.

"This may hurt, I want you to meditate and focus solely on me during this process."

His voice causes goosebumps to litter my exposed skin. Praying he doesn't comment on it, I answer him,

"Yes, Master."

"You can call me Master Brenu if you prefer. This is quite an intimate setting," he mumbles, tying off one end of the thread.

"I prefer Brutis," I smart back.

He hums behind me, "Careful, Lottie. I have a very sharp needle I'm about to pierce you with."

I giggle to myself, proud of irritating the demon-god behind me.

"Deep breath, now. Mediate, focus on my voice," Master instructs.

The large round needle pierces my skin, causing me to grind my teeth to keep from shouting.

"Stay still. Find your peace and listen to me. I am your blam within the storm," he reprimands.

"All dragons of Destrui come from a central god. One that sought love and acceptance for all. He mated with a mortal and thus our creatures were born..."

We stay like this; him relaying the history of our land and creatures. I get lost in the soothing whiskey tones of his voice. It drowns out the burning hot pain shooting through my back, it drowns out every worrisome anxious thought. For the first time I can remember, I am relaxed in the company of a male.

The area along my spine is numb. From the base of my neck to the small of my back.

"And then there was you... The most magnificent of all." The Master finishes his story quietly, letting his fingers drift feather-light over my shoulders.

"Are we done?" I ask, rubbing at my stiff neck.

"Almost. Hollis."

Master's voice barely makes a sound. I look over my shoulder, searching for the male whose name he just spoke when the door before me opens and he comes. Carefully carrying a bowl of water and a stack of white cloths under his arm.

"How did you hear him?" I ask Hollis, confused, still whispering so as not to break the intimacy within the room.

He grins, kneeling down before me.

"You know I can hear everything."

Hollis sets the bowl next to my thigh before taking my hand in his. I watch The Master reach for a cloth before dunking it in the water. The smell of antiseptic rises up, causing me to crinkle my nose.

"This may sting, but I need to heal the wounds and clean the blood from you," The Master drawls out from behind me.

I swallow thickly, bringing Hollis back into my sight.

"Your brand is going to be as lovely as you are."

"Hollis, begin," The Master whispers again.

I watch as Hollis bows his head before speaking quietly.

"I, Hollis Bartek, Guard of the Heir to the Earth Clan, am humbled before you, Scarlett Dea of the Earth Clan. Take this branding as a gift from the gods and use it to serve your purpose. For this is the highest of honors to be chosen by The Master for his vision. My life is yours to serve as you choose. May your reign go on forever."

Tears trickle down my face at his pledge to me. Leaning forward slightly, careful to keep my breast covered, I place a kiss on the crown of his head.

His eyes shine with unshed tears as he looks up.

"Thanks to the gods," The Master mumbles behind me, rinsing the cloth before rubbing my back with it again. His touch is feather soft, barely applying any pressure to the angry flesh.

"Thanks to the gods," Hollis and I whisper in unison, closing out his pledge.

"You're done, Lottie. Go and see the looking glass," Master commands, standing and helping me to my feet. Bowing before me, he extends an arm toward it.

I swallow thickly once more, the impact of this moment washing over me.

Holy goddess. Fuck. Fuck. Fuck. I'm going to be Queen to people who would rather see me dead.

Walking cautiously, my hands pressed to my chest, I turn slightly as I stand before the looking glass. From the nape of my neck almost down to the top of my ass is an intricate threaded "B" with snakes wrapped in flame. Some snakes have dragon wings, some do not. The thread sparkles and shines as I sway back and forth.

"It's beautiful," I breathe out, awe coating my voice. "Thank you."

"It's important," The Master grumbles back.

"Take the compliment, Brutis." I arch an eyebrow at him in the looking glass.

His eyes narrow at me in frustration before commanding, "Hollis, go fetch the handmaids. Scarlett needs to get dressed."

Chapter 11

The bustle of activity around me drowns out any thoughts of what's to come. I'm stripped of my bathing gown roughly. Keeping my back to the wall, I slip on my chemise.

I can't comprehend why I don't want to show off the brand on my back, I just feel like it should remain a secret. Something solely between me and Brutis, it's... intimate.

Every inch of my exposed body is scrubbed with rock salt and lavender, to cleanse and protect me in my new role.

I'm shoved down onto a stool without mercy. A young maid, *Corine I think*, drags the bone comb through my knotted locks, the sound of hair ripping from my scalp loud inside my head.

I'm not allowed to squint or show any sign of discomfort because that would ruin the paste being slathered on my face.

"Hold still, stop wrinkling your nose."

"How do you live with your nails ragged like this? It's disgusting."

Whispers of hope for the females in our clan greet my ears. The many maids surrounding me are excited for this monumental moment in our history.

My mother sweeps into the room, a handmaid behind her carrying the most beautiful dress. It's deep red velvet with pinstripe black stitching. *A reversal of what I've seen the Master's Guard wear.* The skirts billow out, heavy with the expensive fabric. I let my fingers drag over the bodice, taking in the tiny white diamonds decorating the modest sweetheart neckline.

"Since you are the first Queen of our lands, The Master presented you with a gift."

"It's beautiful. Surely, he didn't need to have this made for me," I swallow thickly.

"Be grateful that he is smitten with you, Lottie. Stand, there is only one way in and out of this dress." Mother raises her hand, encouraging me to stand.

On shaking knees, I'm stuck with pins and prodded as I'm sewn into the lavish gown.

Once they've finished situating me, everyone backs away, silence descending upon them. Turning toward the looking glass, I feel the color drain from my face.

Where a young female once stood is a Queen.

I don't recognize this person.

My white hair is braided in large knots hanging over one shoulder. My golden eyes are lined with dark coal and black wax makes my lashes appear longer and thicker. There is gold glitter on my eyes and pink paste coating my cheeks and lips.

It's regal and soft, the expectation of an understated female. Proper, meant to be seen and not heard.

Malinda approaches me, softly pinning white daisies into my hair, following the tail of the braid.

"So you don't forget who you are," she whispers, her eyes filling with tears as she smiles softly.

I lean into her touch for a moment when she cups my cheek. *I love you, Malinda. I am doing this for you, for all of you.*

Straightening, I take in my appearance again.

"I need a moment, everyone out, please."

Turning to look at the room full of females, they bow before me. Bending low at their waist before they turn and leave the room one by one. Only my mother remaining behind. Their show of subservience leaves me uncertain. As though I'm not deserving of their loyalty.

"Scarlett. How do you feel?" her voice is soft, cooing almost, a mother concerned for her child.

"I feel like I could take on the world, Mother."

I straighten my shoulders, clasping my hands in front of me,

"I've spoken to the gods and they've shown me what is to come, what my future holds. I am not afraid. Only determined."

I watch as she attempts to wipe at her tears, before falling to her knees before me.

"Scarlett, if no one else will accept you, know that the females of your Clan will always bow to their Queen."

"With the exception of those in the court." I hold out a hand, lifting her to her feet.

"I love you, Mother," I whisper, wiping her tears with my thumbs.

"And I, you." Her smile is warm as she embraces me, adjusting my flower pins.

The door opens, causing Mother to spin around.

Hollis, Everett, and The Master's Guard are standing outside my door. Hollis and Everett sporting grins of pride while swaggering into the room.

"Don't you both look lovely in your... uniform."

I rake my eyes over the black and red linen covering their bodies.

"It's a special day."

"You both look very handsome," I compliment them, smoothing the cloak covering Hollis's shoulders. "This is much more fitting than your usual brown."

Hollis smiles at me, a peacock preening while Everett's cheeks pink in embarrassment.

"You are beautiful, Scarlett. Allow us to escort the King's daughter one last time."

"Yes, please."

Walking out the door, The Master's Guard lines up, two of them on each side of the hall. Everett holds out his elbow on my left while Hollis repeats the motion to my right. Slipping my hands in, we march, The Master's Guard falling into formation behind us.

Descending the stairs we halt just outside the hall. The Throne Room is full of mortals. A mix of our court and the other royal clans, not one dressed in their finery.

"Good goddess," Hollis grumbles before turning to me.

"We knew there would be protests from the other Clans. We've prepared for it. Are you ready, Scarlett?" he asks, bending low so that we are face to face, his expression fierce and determined.

"I was born for this. Blessed by the gods. I will not be afraid of any mortal."

"That's my Queen." He kisses me on the cheek, Everett bending to do the same.

Over the ruckus inside the Throne Room, my father's announcement rings out.

"Please bow before your Earth Queen. May she reign forever."

Chaos erupts as the Guard leads me inside. Xavier and Louie prevent mortals of the courts from grabbing onto me. I watch as Abel cuts a male's hand off for presenting a vulgar gesture. They are pressing in on all sides, causing The Master's Guard to surround me, a precious stone being carried by the river.

Hollis lets go of me, nodding to Everett before walking in front, ramming his body into a male approaching with a sword.

I keep my face passive at the anarchy breaking out around me. I expected unrest; the brutality these males are exuberating isn't surprising.

A booming echo rings out around the room, causing those rebelling to instantly stop moving and fall to their knees.

The Master of Realms stands at the opposite side entrance, looking directly at me.

He motions us forward with two fingers.

Walking toward him, I look to where my father is seated on his throne. Behind him, regal and breathtaking is my Maxim. I'm desperate to go to him, to be reassured by his strength. He winks at me causing a flutter of love to move through the bond. Standing next to him is my mother, smiling tightly as I approach.

The Master meets us halfway at the foot of the dais, bringing my attention back to the moment.

"Neat trick," I mutter to him, nodding toward the prostate court members.

"We shall call it a *demon* power," he mumbles, holding his hand out to help me onto the platform.

I double-take quickly, a look of surprise crossing my face before I remember to put my mask of indifference back on. The Master takes me from Everett and Hollis, standing me on his right-hand side. Leaning down, he whispers,

"Yes, I know that's what you refer to me as in that pretty little head of yours. Now focus on what we are doing here."

Turning his back on me, he addresses those still on their knees.

"Rise." It comes out quietly, that layered echo working its way across the room.

"I believe in free will, so don't make me do that again," he addresses the crowd.

The mortals seem subdued, their creatures inside of them resting for the moment.

Striding forward, resting at the tip of the dais, he raises his hands,

"I accept this female's lineage and placement on the throne. I will not ask if anyone disputes the heir, as you've made yourselves known."

I watch as some males grumble, making their way toward the open courtyards preparing to shift. I search the crowds for Oz or Malinda, finally making out their smiling faces in the very back of the room. I nod subtly toward them when I notice the Daughters of the Queen standing behind them, all of them serious and regal. Ready for the changes they are desperate for me to invoke. They must have snuck in, determined to show their support.

"Ah, ah, ah," The Master tuts, waving a finger back and forth at those attempting to flee.

"Attendance is mandatory. Don't make me force you back."

The threat rings out around the room, stilling mortals in their place.

"Good. Let's begin the ceremony."

The Master begins telling the history of our beings, how we are all dragons that choose to have mortal skin. We are to obey what our creatures desire, even if it goes against the morals we are taught.

Keeping my features soft, I look around the room surprised by how many females are in attendance wearing looks of disgust as you would a precious gem.

You would think they would see this as a victory, a female to lead. To let them free of their spouses who seek to own them for nothing more than their bodies.

I'm startled out of my observation when The Master takes my hand, a bolt of lightning shooting through my fingers as he eases me into the throne. I situate myself in it, sitting tall and hardening my features.

"King Vika, please pass the crown."

My father kneels before me, a disapproving grimace across his face,

"Should have let your mate be King like I suggested," he whispers to me.

The Master, turning to lift the crown from Father's head pauses, "And go against the very orders I gave you, Vika? I would hope not."

I watch my father's face pale, eyes bouncing back and forth between mine before lowering his hands and heading to the floor in complete submission.

The room is silent, everyone holding their breath and not daring to move as the crown is placed upon my head. It's heavy and I am determined not to waver under the weight of my responsibilities.

"The Earth Queen to your dragons. Let her heal what you have wrecked."

The Master bows deeply to me before wandering off the dais toward the door he came from. No guard to follow him, seemingly without a care in the world.

I rise from my seat, placing a hand on my father's head as I pass.

Stopping at the tip of the dais, I address my Clan.

"The time for fighting is naught within us. We have greater obligations to achieve than to argue over which sex of dragons has the right to reign. I, as your Queen, seek to heal our world before it becomes the death of us."

My heart is racing and I'm beginning to sweat. Bile is rising in my throat, but I have to focus on remaining poised. *I can lose my shit later.*

"Prosperity to Destrui," I announce, bowing my head toward our Clan. When I raise it, I'm not surprised no male rises to greet their leader.

If I was a male they would be falling at my feet and offering to wash them. The Daughters of the Queen immediately begin pushing their way to the front of the room, lining up across the front of the dais and bowing before me. I bow to them before straightening and holding my hand out to the side, palm up. Oz winks at me, a cheeky smile stretching her mouth wide.

Hollis immediately moves forward and takes my hand.

Maxim appears at my side a moment later, taking the other with Everett positioning himself in front of me.

Together we make our way down the aisle, ignoring those losing control over their urges, baring fangs and claws at me.

The council room door echos shut behind me and I fall into the nearest seat, head in my hands.

"That could have gone much worse." Maxim coos, kneeling in front of me.

"Hello, my lovely Queen. I've missed you all day." Peeking through my fingers, I smile back at him.

"What would you like to be your first order of business?" he teases.

I look around, finding Hollis and Everett gone for the moment.

Lifting my eyebrow and dropping my hand, I whisper, "My first order is for you to do that tongue thing again."

His grin grows large, eyebrows lifting as his pupils become pinpricks.

"Right now? Here? You still have to attend the celebration."

"That's not until nightfall. Let's go search out the Queen's chamber, shall we?"

He nods enthusiastically, pulling me excitedly toward the door causing me to trip over my dress.

"We can do so much more than the tongue thing," Maxim suggests, wagging his brows.

"No, we can't. I'm sewn into this, we would have to destroy it to get me out of it."

"Keep the gown on. It'll be my first show of loyalty to the Queen."

Covering my laugh, I let him pull me away from the stress of my life for a little while so we can celebrate this moment.

Chapter 12

"You have to stop disappearing with Max, Scarlett," Hollis admonishes me as he walks me into the Throne Room.

"Rephrase that, Hollis. It really should be 'You have to stop disappearing with Max, *Your Majesty*,'" I quip, smirking at him.

"Yes, Hollis. Make sure you address my Queen correctly," Max adds playfully from behind us.

Hollis scours at him over his shoulder.

"That power is already going to your head, Scar? Good thing you have me here to keep you grounded."

I shake my head at him, hiding my smile behind my hand.

"I think I'll disappear with Max as often as I please," I tease, sitting down on the throne and smiling up at Maxim.

Standing in front of me Hollis shoots a glare at Max, before jesting, "I'm hoping that's because he's figured out how to–"

He cuts himself off, looking toward the doors leading to the courtyard as his body goes tense, claws sprouting from his hands.

"What is it?" I whisper, afraid to speak louder and distract him.

"Maxim. Take Scarlett away. Now."

"What's going on?" Max asks, removing the sword from his side.

"The Royal Courts are coming. Now, Maxim."

Hollis runs toward the courtyard, shifting into a small golden dragon as he does.

"Run, Lottie," Max whispers, tugging my hand.

I'm paralyzed. Dragons are pouring into the Throne Room, hundreds of them. All blue, red, and yellow; clawing at the polished wood floor, scratching along the walls, using their claws to dangle from the torches.

"Let's go!" Max hisses at me, attempting to pull me off the dais.

"No. This was my decision. We knew an uprising was possible and I will not hide from it."

"You'll get yourself killed!"

"Mote it be," I respond, not taking my eyes from The Master's Guard who has entered the room, shifting and launching themselves at the Destrui Dragons.

I can not pull my sight away from the carnage billowing out before me.

The Master's Guards are colors I've never seen. Purple, Orange, Black. Were they not born of a Clan? How do they live together with different morals and customs? Now is not the time to consider life, Scarlett. Get it together!

My eyes catch on Alason, still in his mortal form, standing along a pillar in the shadows, almost hidden from sight.

A male shifts near him, running toward me with a knife held high in his hand. *I will not run, I will not be afraid. This is where I make my stand.*

Letting him jump onto the dais, I hold my hand out touching him lightly on the forehead. Pushing my energy into him, I watch as his body calms before drooping forward slightly.

The few dragons near me take notice, stopping in their biting and ripping to take in the near comatose male at the end of my fingers.

Making eye contact with the closest to me, I beckon him forward.

"You. Shift and state your claim. I will not have this in my home."

The male dragon crunches down on a leg he is carrying in his mouth before snarling at me. His shift is quick, then he's jumping up next to me. Max approaches him with stealth, holding the tip of his sword to his throat.

"Who the fuck are you?" the male spits out at Max.

"Your *Queen's* fucking mate," Max snarls back. "One move and I'll take your head off," he warns the male, eyes blazing.

I reach out my hand toward the mortals and will my energy away from me. The purple mists spread out, covering the floor in a carpet of lavender. It encompasses every mortal, causing eyes to shift toward me.

Sweat is breaking out along my body, dripping down every crevice. I've never tried this on such a large scale and my body is taxing quickly.

"Listen," I command the room.

Nodding to the male next to Max, he begins to speak.

"I've been told to state my claim," he gulps, side-eyeing me before continuing,

"A Queen is out of the question for leadership. Females do not think for themselves, they are not capable of making decisions. Are we going to stand by and do nothing?"

He yells the last part as my energy is slipping away from the crowd. They erupt in roars of agreement.

I nod my head slowly, staring at this brave male.

"How heroic of you, to stand amongst those who are as simple-minded," I state evenly.

Stars are beginning to spot my vision, my energy spent and body on the edge of collapse.

I address those below me,

"I do not lead with fear and violence. It is time to turn away from what we've been taught. If you have an issue, you may address me."

Satisfaction warms me as many begin shifting back to their mortals. Scanning the crowd for Hollis, I sigh in relief as I spot him flying high near the ceiling.

"War, war, war." begins to be chanted throughout the room.

I swallow roughly.

Not the reaction I was hoping for. But then again, when you are raised in a world where death and destruction are ingrained from birth, what else do you expect?

"Grab her!" is shouted from the back of the room.

The chaotic mix of mortal and dragon begins to ascend toward me. I shove the male at my fingertips off the dais into the crowd watching as they swallow him.

The Guard is here in moments, flocking around me as my personal shield.

Adrenaline coursing through me, I grab Max's hand at the same moment I dig my fingers into Hollis's collar with the other.

Understanding my intention, he instantly links hands with Everett. One by one The Masters Guard grabs and bites down on each other.

Closing my eyes and focusing my mind's eye, I drown out the roars and yells racing toward me. Picturing the Cists in my mind, I will myself there. I'm halfway between places when Maxim is ripped from my grasp.

The ground is hard beneath me, my head thudding against the dirt loudly. I watch with blurry vision as my crown bounces twice, rolling through the dirt and into the shelves beyond.

"Goddess, are you okay?" one of the Guard asks me. Either Abel or Alex; I can't remember who is who.

"Let me help you up," he gestures to the others around him. They surround me, grabbing hands and arms to lift me from where I've fallen.

"They took him! They took Max!" I yell, frantically pulling away from them.

I am halfway up the stairs when large rough hands close around my wrist tugging me back down. I pull my arm back, attempting to punch at Everett. I miss, barely skimming his shoulder. My knuckles sting where they scrape over the fabric.

Shaking his head, he hauls me up, carrying me over his shoulder for a few steps before dropping me roughly on the ground next to a shelf of manuscripts.

Crouching down in front of me he holds my head in his hands, squishing my cheeks together.

I glare at him, pissed that he is stopping me from returning for Max.

He shakes his head before turning to look over his shoulder. Following his line of sight, my stomach churns.

The Master's Guard lay on the ground spread out, some still in their dragon form, licking at wounds ripped open on their legs or in their mortals trying to staunch the flow of blood from their abdomens. Everett looks back at me, removing one hand from my face.

He twists his fingers slowly, creating letters in the air.

Wait.

His eyes are hard as they bore into me. Resigned, I nod. My chest is cracking open, splintering in pain wondering what happened to Max.

Everett leans close and kisses my head before standing and rushing over to where Hollis is tying pieces of his cloak around Xavier's leg.

I rise, carefully making my way over.

"We need a healer," I whisper to Hollis.

"Yes. I know that. Thank you for the observation. I'd say to get Oz, but I sent her away to keep her safe," he grounds out, sweat soaking his forehead and shirt.

Feeling helpless, I look around for inspiration. I make my way to the indigo dragon licking at his paw. Bending down, I attempt to take it into my hand when he growls loudly at me.

"Oh, stop that. Let me take a look."

Reaching for it again, I see a piece of a claw stuck in the bottom of his pads.

My mouth screws up as I consider how best to remove it. I set it down carefully, running a hand along his large head.

"I'll be right back. Leave it alone, don't lick it," I instruct, turning my back on him.

The souls of the library are floating near the ceiling, watching our wounded with interest. I beckon to one, coaxing it to come down.

Bouncing softly down on an invisible current, it lands in my palm.

"Hello, beautiful. I need some help."

Turning the soul toward the males littering the floor, I whisper, "Do you have any reading on healers? Something I could use to help?"

The soul turns bright orange before lulling back to its sunny yellow. Floating up and away, I follow curiously through the stacks. Going deeper and deeper within the library until it stops in front of a small faded black leather book.

Reaching for it, it is swiped out of my reach.

Turning I see Everett holding it open, eyes running quickly through the pages.

He must find what he is looking for because his eyes meet mine before nodding over his shoulder.

I follow him back watching him turn pages faster than it can be possible to read.

He veers off down another stack as I continue my way back to the Guards.

Approaching the indigo dragon, I admonish him,

"I told you not to lick that."

He whines faintly before snorting at me.

Examining his paw again, I reach up and remove a daisy pin from my hair. Moving carefully I wedge it under the jagged piece of a claw, pushing lightly until it starts to pull up, tearing the pad in the process. The dragon snaps at me, before pulling back and lowering his head.

"I'd smack you for that, but I'm not exactly sure which Guard you are and Abel scares me," I tease, trying to ease his discomfort.

The claw finally pops free. Blood pouring out in its wake. Ripping the bottom of my skirt, I press it tightly to the wound, soaking up the blood.

Tying it off, I stand looking around. Two others still lay on their side.

Everyone's distracted. I can leave to get Max. They won't notice.

Just as the thought enters my mind, I push it away. *I haven't felt pain or suffering through the bond. Surely, if he was being hurt, I would know.*

Renewed determination drives me, I bandage and soothe as best I know how. Once everyone is situated and resting, Everett comes clambering back in holding a small pot and vials.

I eye him, "Where did you get those? I've scoured every inch of this library. I know it like the back of my hand."

Everett rolls his eyes at me, giving me a look I take to mean "obviously not."

He sets his finds down on top of one of the Cists, with complete disregard for the bodies they hold.

Opening the small bound book, he points to a page.

Looking over it, I can't read it. *It's all symbols I haven't seen before.*

Everett begins pouring liquids from the vials into the pot. Stirring it with his finger every so often. I watch as it smokes and pops, fascinated. He takes my hand and quickly scores the palm with a blade. I cry out against the sting, pulling my hand back toward me, but he doesn't let it go. Holding it over the small pot, he squeezes until my blood drips in steadily.

The smoking and fizzing cease instantly. His warm wet tongue sneaks out and quickly licks the blood pooling on my palm before dropping it. The aroma from the pot reminds me of ambrosia. Enticing and alluring.

Everett stalks toward Hollis sitting on the floor, head hanging between his knees. Tapping him on the shoulder, Everett presents him with the pot.

A gesture from Everett and Hollis is tilting it back, swallowing loudly.

Everett repeats this with every member of the guard, saving himself for last. The guard settles, the remaining changing back into their mortal beings. Everyone lies across the floor chatting, serene and calm.

Finding courage in this strange situation, I make my way to Hollis and Everett, both leaning against each other with small smiles on their faces.

"What did you give them?" I ask Everett, sitting crossed-legged in front of them.

Hollis answers for him, "A healing potion mixed

with some of your blood, Your Goddess-ness. They will be fit in no time."

His words are slurred slightly, looking at him closer he almost appears drunk. Not fully, but like he's been partaking.

I study Everett, he wears the same expression as Hollis, dreamy and untethered. Slowly one by one, the Guards fall into slumber.

I watch them dreaming for some time, hoping they will wake soon.

I guess since no one else is worried sick over my mate, I'll go find him myself.

I close my eyes, trying to find the bond tethering us together inside of me. I focus on the spot where it should be inside my head, feeling nothing but panic.

Chapter 13

I consider briefly walking up the stairs, but I don't want to wake them and be stopped again. Standing, the room spins around me. Holding on to the shelf to steady myself, I attempt to focus my mind. Forcing the image of my chamber into existence.

I will myself to dissipate, to jump there, but nothing happens. My body is worn and tired, begging me to rest.

That is not going to happen right now, I can sleep when I find Max. He can sleep with me, safe and sound.

I smile to myself, picturing his face relaxed in slumber.

Taking a few deep breaths, I dig deep within myself. Pulling up energy from low in the well deep inside me. It's faint, just barely a puddle left, a raindrop compared to an ocean.

I picture it floating up, washing slowly over my body. Once it reaches my hands, I wave my fingers over my face. The pull outwards is cold and soundless. My eyes open and I'm standing in my chamber.

Dizzy, I catch myself against the bedpost for a moment before righting myself.

"I was wondering when you would appear."

I spin quickly at the sound of my father's voice.

"Father!" I scramble toward him, landing on my knees before him.

"You have to help! Maxim has been taken in the raid. We must find him," I plead, tears running down my face.

"Yes, that is unfortunate," he mumbles, running his fingers through my mused hair lovingly before continuing,

"What is even more unfortunate is that The Master was wrong. This is a sign from the gods, a female is not meant to lead."

Bile rises in my throat, causing me to cough before I manage to croak out, "Father. It hasn't even been a day, surely–"

"No, it hasn't even been a day. And look at what has happened. A raid on my castle, on my very throne. Your mate has been taken hostage and the other Clans are burning our females as we speak."

My head swings to the side, attempting to see out of the windows next to us.

Oz... Malinda...

He continues in his slow, even tone,

"The universe, the fates themselves, do not want you as Queen. The Master can stake me through the heart if he likes, but this will be for the best." He drops his hand into his lap, staring at a spot over my shoulder.

"We should have listened to Alason. Females shouldn't lead, Scarlett. You exist to be bedded and bred. That is the way it has always been."

Silence fills the room as tears burn their way down my face.

"And as for your mate... Maxim will have to go, as well. There is something wrong with him. You see, I spoke to him just moments ago. He seems deranged, talking about the realm ending and there being a way to leave it. I don't need insanity being bred into your offspring."

My heart stops beating, my stomach drops and turns sour. The seconds crawl by before I manage to whisper,

"Max isn't deranged, Father. You said yourself that our world needs healing. Alason even wanted to sacrifice me to Aether to buy our favor!"

"We do need healing," he replies, stroking a finger down my face and catching a teardrop. "I'm not taking sides, but I am taking control."

He rubs the tear between his forefinger and thumb, shaking his head sadly.

"From this moment forward, you are not to leave your chambers until I decide how best to proceed."

"Father!" I cry outraged.

"You heard me. You've forgotten your place within this court. I will take the blame for that. I followed Master Brenu's order but it has done nothing but harm those we are responsible for."

He untangles my hands that have twisted themselves in the velvet of his robes, brushing the fabric out as he stands. The door slams behind him, the lock clicking into place.

I crumble to the floor, scratching my nails into the wood beneath me. I can't breathe, I can't see. The sobs wringing from my chest have no sound behind them, a silent desperate plea.

The door creaks open, letting in a small sliver of light before closing again quickly.

The rug beneath my face is rough, scratching the raw skin there. I'm staring into what remains of the fire, long since having died out.

"Get off the floor child," small hands lift me, pulling under my shoulders and forcing me up.

Mother pulls me into a sitting position, leaning me against the sitting chair.

I stare at her, unblinking. Her dark brown hair coffined smartly. Her eyes have bruises forming under them. Her mouth is nothing more than a grim line, pinched tight.

There is nothing left for me to fight for. Maxim is taken from me. My title has been stripped.

Slowly, I fall into her lap, a youngling seeking her mother's comfort. She runs her hands over my hair smoothing the matted braid. It's soothing, comforting me in this dark place I have found myself in.

"Shh, Scarlett," she coos, wiping a cool rag along my face. *I didn't realize I was crying.* I bury my face into her skirts to hide the tears that won't stop flowing.

"I worried this would happen when The Master decreed it. A female ruling this land. Look what's happened." Her voice is soft, resigned. I feel her body shake slightly under me.

My voice cracks as I attempt to speak, the sound muffled by my hidden face.

"I know what you're going to say. A female is meant to be owned by a male, not the other way around."

I roll off her lap and back down onto the rug. I have no will to continue the mundane scolding I've heard all my life.

She doesn't force it, quietly getting up to leave. Her back is to me, hand on the doorknob when she stops.

"I was sent to inform you that there are to be no visitors. Your Guard has been retired from his post and there will be a vote by the Kings on how to deal with you."

Her voice breaks on the last word. A small sob escapes before she hurries out, the lock clicking into place.

I drag myself over, crawling against the wood floor, using the knob on the door as leverage, I stand and begin banging with the side of my fists.

"Hollis! Everett. Anyone– let me out. I demand to be let out!"

I scream it over and over again, my voice raw and hoarse. The sides of my hands are raw and bleeding from the abuse.

The sobs overtake me as I fall to the floor, scraping my nails along the wood, blood staining the door in long streaks.

"You can't do this–they can't." My voice is a whisper, having long since given out.

I bang on the door for hours until my body caves in on itself, exhaustion finally taking over.

A tapping on my balcony window has me glancing toward it. In the dead of night, no light emerges. Even the moon has turned its back on me.

The tapping starts again. Slowly I drag myself over to it. Through the dark glass, golden eyes flash at me.

Scurrying, I try the handle. Cursing when I find it welded shut. The gold eyes watch me for a moment, holding a finger to his lips.

"Hollis," I cry, tears streaming down my face.

He holds his hand to the glass and I press my palm against it. The glass is cold beneath it, fog forming around the warmth.

His mouth is moving, and I can just barely make out his words.

"I have to leave, it isn't safe for you if I stay. I'll be back soon."

My face crumbles and any hope I had that he was coming to save me disappears.

"Everett is here. He will protect you." Pressing his forehead against the glass, he sobs harshly before disappearing back into the darkness.

Straining my eyes, I try to make out his retreating form in the darkness, barely making out his shift and flight into the sky.

"Bring me with you!" I desperately whisper into the glass.

At least he's safe. I hope wherever he seeks refuge will be kind to him.

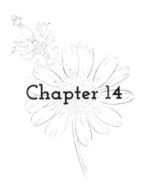

Chapter 14

The knock at my door is sudden, causing me to jump up from where I fell asleep in front of the patio's glass doors. It's still dark out, the sun not even hinting at shining. A perfect landscape for the despair I find myself in.

Mother pushes open the door, her head hanging from her shoulders in defeat.

"You are being summoned."

I swallow thickly, my heart racing at her words. Sweat is beginning to cover my brow. I follow her through the hall, the King's guards on every side of me, dressed in brown leather matching their dragons' scales.

Where did The Master's Guard go? Home, I'm sure, after my failed attempt at ruling.

My mother stops outside the door to the Throne Room. Her voice is barely more than a whisper.

"I'm sorry I've failed to protect you. I'm not allowed in. Go."

Her shoulders shake violently, but no sound of crying leaves her.

Keeping my eyes drawn to the floor, I make my way slowly toward the dais.

"The judgment has been decided," Alason's voice ringing out has my breath stalling in my lungs.

The room breaks out in applause, I peek enough to the side that I can see the court and the other clans' Royal Courts positioned around us.

"Kneel, Scarlett. The Destrui Kings have decided your fate. The kindest thing we could do is banishment. We believe you used curses from the gods to convince King Vika to appoint you Queen. A disgrace to your sex."

He mumbles the last part attempting to appear somber but his glee creeps through as a smile lights up his voice.

My curses from the gods? If I had the power to control the will of others then I would be a god, not a mere mortal subjected to a life where I live in service to males.

The males of the courts announce their agreement. Cheers ring out from the long table next to the dais. Lifting my head, my gaze locks on King Clayen. The only Destrui King that has bothered to show himself for my sentencing. His face is somber, staring at me. Subtly he shakes his head at me, tapping his finger to his lips.

His reaction is odd. What is he trying to tell me? Did he not agree to this?

Alason's voice causes my gaze to fly to him.

"You are not to return, under any circumstance."

"I didn't use magic on anyone! This was Master Brenu's idea, why can't you see that?"

Defiance blooming through my veins, I lift to my feet, staring up at him.

Alason sits on the throne, crown lopsided on his head wearing Father's robe and furs.

Where is Father? Alason has his royal cloaks...

"I may believe that," Alason muses, "you may believe that. But the other Clans do not. A powerful female will only bring down our world. That is evident in your miserable hours attempting to lead. You will be wiped from our histories."

I stare him down, defiance burning in my soul. My face heats, the tears drying instantly.

"You may try to banish me, but I am the daughter of King Vika, the rightful heir according to The Master of Realms. How do you plan on explaining my banishment to him?"

Alason squints down at me, appearing to contemplate my statement before laughing harshly.

"His Guards have been sent away. Told that you had run from your duties. They'll report that to The

Master and there will be no trouble. Master Brenu approved this punishment and voted for it himself."

Alason's grin turns feral, his glee breaking through.

"But there is still the matter of *your* Guard we have to address, Scarlett."

The sound of a struggle booms from my left, seven of the king's guards drag Everett into the room, hands bound behind his back and tangled in heavy chains.

Eyes wide, my head swings back toward Alason.

"What is the meaning of this?" I hiss, "Release him. Now."

"No, I don't think I will. Everything associated with you has already been taken care of. If you were allowed to venture outside the walls of this keep, you would notice the females who supported you are dead and strung up by their feet, left to rot. We painted *Daughter of the Queen* on each one. Painted quite a picture."

My stomach rolls, threatening to expel the bile swimming in my stomach. Visions of rotting corpses with birds picking out their eyes fill my mind.

"Your handmaid, Malinda, was it? She put up quite a fight. I gave her to my guard so they could break her in. Don't worry, she's not alone in her penance, I sent Oz with her."

His smile is depraved as he thoughtfully twists his hair around his finger. The guards holding Everett laugh loudly while those of the Royal Courts bang their goblets against the table in support.

Those males aren't my father's Guard. I've never seen them. Mal, Oz... my loving, sweet...

"As for Everett, I like him. He's quiet. Has good drive and discipline. I want to keep him as my Guard. He will be an asset, but he too needs to pay his price for participating in your crimes."

Everett grunts loudly as his head is placed in the small pillory. Alason slowly pushes himself from his seat. Striding toward the massive fireplaces, he takes an iron brand from the fire, observing it for a moment before walking toward Everett's heaving, struggling form.

He holds it out to me, glowing red and angry.

"This design is special, perhaps you've seen it before? The predators' mark. Means he's too dangerous to ever be trusted—a plague on his mortal, a rapist, an abuser. Shame really, no one will ever come near him. Except me of course, but that's for my own amusement."

Turning quickly on his heel, Alason presses the brand down into the side of Everett's face before I can even force a breath into my lungs.

The smell of scalding flesh hits me like an arrow to my core. I double over as sobs rack my body, and for the first time in my life hear Everett's voice, begging for mercy. Begging for his death.

I run, desperately wanting to save my gentle giant from his fate. Throwing myself across him, I watch as the blistering skin bubbles. The skin is already starting to peel off in layers across his face. Sobbing violently, I whisper to him, "I'm sorry. I'm sorry. I'll make it right for you. I swear. This is my fault. I'll kill th-"

I'm dragged roughly off of him, thrown to the floor landing on my back. Everett is dragged from the room, his body deathly still.

I pray to the goddess he passed out from the pain and won't remember it.

It's a useless prayer, but I hope somehow, someone above hears it.

"All he ever did was be my friend!" I spit out, attempting to bring my energy to the surface. It feels as though a stone block is sitting on top of the well that holds my magic, and no matter how hard I try I can't budge it out of the way.

"Lead Scarlett out," Alason dismisses me, flicking his fingers.

"I need to convene with my guard and the clans to determine where we are sending her," Alason mutters softly, absently wiping his fingers on his clothes with his back to me, bored with the abuse he has doled out.

Fingers dig into my upper arm, pinching the tender flesh there as I'm dragged from the room.

I'm handed off to my mother, waiting just outside the room. Head still bowed in subservience, she takes my hand, tenderly running her thumb along it.

"Dry your tears, Scarlett. Don't let them see you fall."

My head snaps toward her and for the first time, I notice how much she has aged. *Worn down and beaten by her place within this court.*

"I will do what needs to be done for my Clan. For those who have had their voices beaten out of them."

I drag her to me, embracing her on the stairs. I squeeze her tightly. Kissing her ear, I let her go as a guard pulls me away. Fighting off his grip, I stride toward my chamber, leaving her staring after me.

Females should not bow to males. I slam the chamber door behind me. The Guard clicks the lock into place.

Good. Lock me in. I can just dissipate out and get to Everett, then go find Max.

Closing my eyes, I focus. Determined to bring myself from this place. Nothing happens, not even a spark of energy. It feels trapped within me.

Okay, so no magic. I'll just have to figure something else out.

I look toward the bathing chamber considering if the hot water will help wash off the day.

Rising, I make my way over, I set the water to heat over the small flame left in the hearth. Slowly pouring the water in, I attempt to steady my shaking hands and pull at the bodice of my gown.

Glancing down at it when it refuses to budge, *Oh right, I was sewn into the ascendance gown, it can't just be taken off.*

Hiking up the skirts, I step inside the tub, the layers of velvet and silk, billowing out around me. I get a vision of drowning it, ruining the dress the way I have been.

I sit slowly, pushing the fabric down until the water is overfilling the tub, pouring out onto the floor around me. Willing my claws to protrude I stand, I rip through the bottom layers of the gown, letting it stop just short of the top of my thighs. The jagged material uneven and scratchy against my legs.

Smiling to myself, I claw at the material until only the bodice holding my breasts up remains.

Dropping the sopping wet fabric, it plops to the floor and I sink back into the scalding water.

I could drown myself.

I shake off the intrusive thought, careening my head back and forth. The movement pulls at the flower pins in my hair.

Reaching up, I remove them one by one. Holding them in my palms, I study them for a moment—dainty daisies made from silver and gold. The only adornment ever befitted me that was created solely for my pleasure.

Clutching them for a moment, I let the sharp pins stab into my hands, then very carefully shove them down my bodice, nestled in between my breasts.

I never know when I might need a weapon.

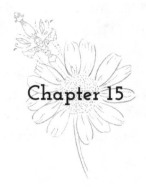

Chapter 15

Days go by, the hours and minutes blending in together until I can't tell one from the other. My mind is falling into a dense fog. Each day becoming murkier than the last, like trying to wipe water drops from a window.

The mating bond is fading as does the fog lifting at the sight of the morning sun. My friends are either missing or dead and there is no end in sight for me. The only being allowed in and out of my room is Mother.

She's not encouraging and hopeful as she used to be; instead, remorseful and withdrawn going through the motions of her duties instead of enjoying them as she once did.

"Mother, what if Max is dead?" I whisper out the hidden thought residing deep within my soul.

"Stop worrying and let me get you out of those rags."

I rub at the spot Max bit me the first time we were together. The ridges from his teeth are long since gone. Ignoring her hundredth attempt to get me to change clothes, I respond, "I feel the bond fading, it prickles inside my head. Like an itch I can't scratch. My soul and heart ache so badly, I feel as though I'm going crazy." I whisper my confession, unable to look her in the eye.

She bends down in front of me, forcing herself into my space.

"Nonsense, Lottie, bonds aren't in your head. They're in your heart, your very soul. It's just because you are separated. Most will go crazy without their lovers by their side. You shouldn't worry about that though."

I consider her words a moment. Hearing what she doesn't say: I'll be gone soon anyway.

That makes sense, bonds can bend and stretch, never truly breaking. There was a cautionary tale as a child, that to reject one's mate wouldn't even sever the bond. One would have to die to rid the other of the pain of being bonded but never together.

"Where is he? Have you heard anything?" hope begins to bloom in my chest. The maids love to gossip, surely, she's heard something. I picture Max's face in my mind, that carefree grin and his playful ways fraught with mood swings.

"Naught. I'm not told much these days. We've been forbidden from speaking," Mother retorts.

I scratch at the place in my mind where I imagine the bond being. Trying desperately to follow it to Max, to get even a glimpse of emotion. Nothing, a desert of emptiness and despair greets me. It feels weathered and old like if I fiddle with it it'll break at any moment.

"Is Everett still around?" I ask, getting up and wandering to the windows overlooking the castle grounds.

"Aye," she whispers, placing a hand on my back.

"Can you send him to me?" I turn toward her, staring her in the eye.

"I'll try, Scarlett."

"That is all I ask."

Mother wrings her fingers together, watching me warily.

"I wonder if I shouldn't have him fetched; you've caused so much trouble lately. Wouldn't it be better to quietly wait out your sentence? To go quietly where they choose to send you and live out the rest of your days in peace?"

And she calls herself my mother? Does she not know me at all? Do I ever do anything that I'm ordered to?

My face must speak my thoughts loudly because she backtracks quickly, moving the conversation back to my appearance.

"Child, please let me bathe and dress you. Your gown is ripped to shreds, something else would be more comfortable and modest."

I tilt my head at her, admiring her thorough process. Ever the dutiful female that she is.

"Mother, haven't you ever wanted more in life?"

"Yes, and I thought I had it the day you were crowned. But now there are whispers that you are a traitor amongst our kind. Using magic not known to mortals in order to control those around you."

My face hardens at her words. *Surely this lie hasn't been spread to everyone I've ever known. A disease spread by males afraid of their own egos.*

"Consider these scraps the uniform of a female scorned, locked away with her innocence to prove. You can remove them from my corpse.

"All I ever wanted was to help our world; to heal the lands. Yet, I am banished as a traitor. While those who encourage deceit are celebrated."

I watch her face turn ashen at my words. She steps away from me quickly, "I'm just trying to help you, Scarlett."

"No, you've proven your loyalty. If you truly supported me you'd be hanging with the female commoners along the palace walls. Instead, The Daughters of the Queen are left to rot. Dying for wanting more from their pathetic existence. They will never get a chance to make any changes, to see their sacrifices mean something.

"Malinda is gone, the only real mother I ever had and here you are, attempting to stand in her place. You are a disgrace to her legacy."

I can feel my temper rising, blood rushing to my face. Balling my hands into fists, I turn from her, letting my matted hair twirl out around me.

"I am loyal." Her voice shakes with the conviction of her lies.

"To Alason. To the Kings of Destrui. Not to me; not to my loyalist whose corpses lie rotting in the heat. Get out, Mother. And please, do not return."

Tears spill down her cheeks, but all she does is nod before fleeing my presence.

Determination scalds my veins. I stand at the door for hours, banging against it. I throw bowls and basins across the room, satisfaction raining down with every piece that shatters on impact. The cracking sound brings a wild grin to my face.

Delirious in my rage, I yell for the entire Clan to hear me. Selecting a sitting chair and dragging it toward the balcony windows, I pick it up, smashing the wooden legs against the glass over and over, until it shatters, raining a storm of glass.

Alason's guards stand on the balcony with arrows pointed. I hiss at them before turning around quickly, striding toward my bed.

Considering the sheets and pillows, I let myself shift.

The large creature takes over, not quite fitting within my chamber. I heave my massive body into the bed, holding a pillow down with my paw while tearing at it with my teeth. Feathers spill out as an idea pops into my mind. I shake my head violently, trying to subdue my prey. They fly softly through the air, covering the room in soft down.

The sheets get a similar treatment as I tear at them with my claws. Looking around, I let my creature determine what she wants to do next. She focuses on the bathing room. I let her take the reins, giving into nature. My mortal mind overseeing the destruction with approval. A swing of her tail and the tub is knocked to its side. The closet tipped over. The dragon grips my clothes in her maw, shredding them before nesting down inside the ruin.

On a whim of curiosity, she lets out a ring of fire. A special trick to my creature. Not every dragon breathes fire, especially those born to the Earth Clan.

Disappointment flows through her as it only chars the objects around, not truly creating the blaze she hoped for.

Taking back control from the creature, I ball up in the shreds of my clothes, huffing quietly as I seek out Max again. The bond is slowly fading, brittle and broken inside of me. I get a flash of pity in my belly, just for a moment. It's an unwelcome feeling and I push it away. Shifting back into my mortal form, I attempt to sleep.

The door creaks as Alason peeks his head into my chambers before pushing it open fully.

Hands planted on his hips, he spins slowly.

"This is a mess. You've done a fine job destroying everything that was ever given to you, entitled silly female."

I watch as he continues to take in the shredded chamber. Feathers and cloth litter the room, the stone walls bearing claw marks. The blackened soot underfoot proof that this castle had been hilt with dragons in mind.

I stand from my nest, pushing my greasy strands back out of my face, proud at my fit of rage.

My hand tangled in my braid, I stare through him, not quite acknowledging his presence.

"Why hasn't Father come to speak to me about it? Or at least Mother?"

"They are currently... indisposed. Nothing you need to worry about."

Alason has my full attention now, my eyes flying to his. I scrutinize him, watching him fiddle with his cloak and the dagger at his side.

"You have to forgive me, Scarlett," he sighs.

I settle myself back into my nest of ripped gowns and skirts, looking around the remnants of the chamber slowly before demanding,

"Where is Maxim? I'm assuming he's still alive, I can feel the bond stretching. Brittle, but still there."

He rubs his earlobe for a moment, "He's been taken care of."

"He's dead," I state, looking for any detection of a lie.

He smiles, deadly amusement caressing his features.

I settle myself back along the rubble that was once my chambers and watch him curiously. He crouches on the ground in front of me, appearing to struggle with whatever it is he wants to say. He takes a deep breath, opening and closing his mouth in quick succession.

Finally, he chooses his words, "I was told you've been asking for Everett.

"If you calm down for a bit, maybe stop destroying everything around you, I'll consider letting him see you. He's been detained in the dungeons for a while. I'm sure he'd love to stretch his legs."

I don't answer him, don't even acknowledge his statement in fear that he is dangling a prize in front of me, baiting me to react just so he can snatch it away.

I wave him away carelessly, resting my eyes, too tired to play his game.

The morning light is barely gracing the horizon when the door to my chamber opens.

Alason stands in the doorway, motioning a hulking figure inside.

I sit up quickly, rubbing my eyes as I'm sure I'm hallucinating.

"As you requested. I figured it wouldn't hurt considering he can't say anything to you. Mutism benefits those who need secrets kept. Enjoy the pus oozing from his face."

My eyes widen at Alason's harsh words and I watch Everett cut his eyes toward him, a flash of yellow lightning piercing his dark brown eyes for a moment.

"Everett, see if you can get her to get out of that bed, and perhaps bathe." Alason waves a hand at me before walking out of the room, locking it behind him.

I run to my friend, the only friendly soul I have encountered in days. Attempting to wrap my arms around his middle, I squeeze with everything I have.

Looking up at him, he smiles softly back at me, rubbing the back of this finger down my face. His brand is a blistering and oozing infection, the skin turning black. Tears form anew as I quietly ask, "Are you okay?"

He nods quickly, waving off my concern.

"Is Hollis alright?"

He smiles, squeezing me tight.

"Please, Everett, you have to help me. Max is dead. I know he is, I can't feel anything anymore. I know I sound crazy, but that's the only thing I can come up with!"

He shakes his head at me, holding up his hands in confusion.

"Mating bonds are supposed to be about love. I should be able to feel him, to hear him, right? Yet, all I have is a useless stretch taking up space in my brain." I spit out through the tears coating my lips.

"Please. It's causing me to lose all desire to do anything. I can't eat, drink, or sleep," I beg, falling onto my hands and knees, sobbing.

"If I try to go against what the bond wants it snaps me like a rubber band. I'm begging you to help me! Please! If you love me at all… I know I have no right to ask anything of you considering what I've put you through."

His face is tormented, pain and anger radiating from his powerful form. Grabbing me on each side of my head, he begins shaking me violently before reaching under my arms and dragging me across the room with him.

Propping me upright against him, he points out the window next to my bathing chamber, toward the area where the forest meets the mountains.

I look at him in confusion before looking back out. Rubbing the tears from my face, I try to focus on what he's telling me.

Holding my hands up, I spin on him,

"What? It's the mountains."

He rubs his hand down his face in frustration before pointing again and connecting his little fingers, opening and closing his palms on a hinge. I shrug, not understanding. Rolling his eyes, Everett walks away from me, pacing the small room.

Finally, he stops, annoyance marring his expression then crinkles his nose before reaching into the back pocket of his trousers. Hidden beneath his cloak, he removes a small book. He turns slightly from me, but not before I get a glimpse of the cover.

"You think now is a good time to read a lover's manuscript, Everett?" laughter threatens to bubble up inside of me.

His lips curl up at me as he flips through, walking over he holds it out, one thick finger pointing to the page.

"The magic he had in his trousers made her want to combust—"

"I'm not sleeping with you and this is not the time for that!" I shriek at him, before falling into a fit of laughter that has me clutching my sides. It cleanses some of the torment from my soul.

"Why are you carrying that around? Do you read that?" I snort my amusement.

Rolling his eyes to the heavens and releasing a deep breath, he points to the sentence again, tapping one word over and over.

"Magic," I say aloud. "Magic. Holy dragonshit, *I have magic?"*

Everett hits himself in the forehead making a "duh" face at me.

"How the actual fuck did I forget I had magic? Must be the grief." I throw my hands into the air, "Don't you think I've tried that already? I can't use it," I sneer at him.

He points out the window again to the forest and the mountains.

"The library," I whisper. "*That* magic. How do we get there?"

There is a gentle tug on my hand. Looking toward Everett, he holds up a finger signaling me to be quiet.

Dropping my hand, he grabs my shoulders and positions me slightly away from him.

He rears back, his fist creating a hole in the glass of the window. Pulling it slowly out, he examines the blood pouring from his cuts, picking large chunks of glass out of his skin. Before reaching back in, knocking the rest to the floor.

He climbs out, barely squeezing his massive shoulders through the narrow opening.

Holding on to the ledge, balancing his feet on the concrete ridges of the roof, he motions me forward.

Running toward him, I limber out. Tearing the bodice of my gown in the process.

Once I'm situated next to him, he shifts his dragon flying into the sky, roaring his freedom. Not wasting time I follow him, gliding into the early morning sun.

Chapter 16

We land with a thud against the soft dewy ground, the scorched dying earth prominent amidst the patches of green grass. Shifting back, I take only a moment to look around before making my way to the hidden door in the ground.

Everett beats me there, rolling back the sod and heaving open the door. He jumps in first and I follow quickly after him.

The familiar smell of old and damp welcomes me. The darkness a stark contrast to the blistering sun above the ground. Not giving myself time to adjust, I begin marching toward the Cists, running my fingers along the shelves as I look for the grimoire.

It calls to me like a siren in the night bidding me forward.

My fingers rake over the binding, sending a spark of recognition into my soul. Heaving it down from where it lies above my head, I place it on top of the nearest Cist, the heavy book thudding in the silence.

"Everett," I call out and he's at my side in moments, "Talk some things through with me. "

He nods, watching as I absently thumb through the pages.

"This grimoire holds secrets not known to this world. I only know of it because I saw it in a dream once..." I trail off, remembering the vivid hell-walk from when I was a child.

"I'm going to ask it to reveal my secrets, I need you to ground me so I don't get lost."

His face is grim as he nods at my request. Letting my fangs emerge, I bite down into the soft flesh of my palm and bleed onto the pages, offering a blood pledge in place of my magic. The pages begin flipping quickly of their own will. I feel light emitting from my eyes and mouth before I'm absorbed in its teachings.

The embroidery tattoo greets me, a mirror image of mine done in bright white thread on a large male's back. He feels vaguely familiar, but it's fleeting before I'm dragged into an image of Maxim, kissing me softly before laying me on a bed in slumber, blood coating his hands. I watch my magic leave my body, absorbing into Alason. He takes me from Max, laying me out in a bed of white flowers: roses, daisies, carnations. I'm beautiful in my slumber until he places me on an altar and stabs a dagger through my heart.

A female with blue hair appears before me, her large eyes black and soulless. Tiny dragons fly in them, around and around in a perfect circle, like dolls tied to a string. I stare into them, getting lost in the mechanical movement.

"The male who saves you returns."

It screeches into my ears, causing me to cower and cover them against her shrieks.

Strong hands shake me roughly, my head rolling on my shoulders. Everett's shape slowly begins to form in front of me. He angrily claps the book shut, slamming it on the nearest shelf.

His face is fuming, smoke pouring from his ears as he crouches down in front of me. Reaching up, he plucks me hard between the eyes.

"Guess I got a little lost?" I ask, trying to grin at him. My attempt to lighten the situation doesn't work, instead, he plucks me in between my eyes again, scowling at me.

Rubbing at the spot, I pout.

"Alason took my magic, I don't know how but I saw him absorbing it."

His scowl falls at my words, turning into concern. Running his hands along my back, he stills briefly over the tattoo.

A creak causes me to tense, attempting to look around Everett's shoulder. He squeezes me softly, before rising. Seconds later, I'm tackled to the ground.

"I've missed you. Thank goddess you're okay," Maxim mumbles, kissing my face repeatedly.

"Max!"

I can't get any more words out as I bask in his affection, watching in my mind as the bond solidifies back into place.

Instead of joy radiating from it, there is a feeling of remorse banging within my chest.

Choosing to ignore the intruding emotion, I focus on the exhilaration radiating in my bond, giving in to the overwhelming love Max bestows upon me.

"Let's get you out of the dirt," he mumbles, face buried in the hair at my neck.

"Would be easier if you got off of me," I tease.

"But it's my happy place. You are my happy place." Max sighs deeply, crushing me into the ground under his weight.

Jumping up, he pulls me with him. "Hurry, come with me. I need you all to myself for a moment."

He pulls me through the library, away from the Cists and Everett. Through stacks and tunnels until we reach a long hall. He guides me quickly toward the door on the far end, ushering me in.

"Is this new? I've never seen it before."

He doesn't answer me, instead, his hands rake over my matted hair, before bringing his vision lower.

"My gods, Scarlet. What are you wearing?"

I finger the dirty, ragged material. "My ascendance gown. It's much better like this, don't you agree?"

"It needs to be burned." He grins before pulling me roughly towards him again.

I let him kiss me, thoroughly overcome when his tongue darts into my mouth.

"Where have you been?" I whisper, trying to pull back.

"Later, later. I need you. Now. I've been so worried."

He walks me back toward a bed, laying me down on it roughly. Not even bothering to attempt to uncover my skin, he pushes up what remains of my skirts, never removing his lips from mine. Reaching down, my fingers fumble with the buttons of his pants.

There has got to be a better design for these things.

My body is burning for him, begging me to hurry up. He wastes no time, tearing my bloomers down my legs quickly.

Max shoves in roughly, causing me to call out in pain.

"I'm sorry. Slow, slow," he chants to himself, attempting to slow his pace. He's so overcome with emotion that he can't. Pulling me up toward him, he lays back, reversing our positions.

"I can't do slow, you'll have to do it."

I stare at him perplexed. *Surely this isn't how it's done.*

He grabs my hips, moving them side to side. "Just do what feels right, stop thinking and just do."

Closing my eyes, I concentrate on that. *Up and down, spin, wiggle. Up and down.* Max removes his hands as I find my pace, letting them rest above his head. I press one hand down to his chest, giving myself leverage. My movements become frantic over him, my eyes opening slightly, taking in Max biting his lip, brows knit in concentration.

Rearing up suddenly so that we are nose to nose, he holds my hips up, pounding into me.

He bites into my neck, that same agonizing pleasure radiating through me. As he does, I begin toeing the edge of that cliff.

I collapse on top of Maxim, breathing hard,

"Shit."

"What?" he asks between panted breaths.

"You weren't meant to hear that," I whisper, hiding my face in his shirt.

Huh, he never got around to taking this off.

I breathe deep, taking in his unique musk.

"What is 'shit' supposed to mean?

"Oh. Just, you know. I didn't get to- Only with your mouth have I been able to..."

My hand is twisting in the air as I refuse to look at him.

He chuckles low, "Told you it takes practice."

I cuddle into him a moment longer, then he is rolling me off of him. Standing from the bed, he hoists his pants back on, staring at me.

I suddenly feel alone and cold, not at all the warm reunion I have been wishing for.

"You need to change clothes. Would you like a bath?" he asks tenderly, affection blooming in his eyes.

"Yes, but let's talk first."

"Okay," he draws out, slowly.

"I've been so worried. Alason told me you were dead. Where have you been?"

He blushes crimson, a scalding color across his face.

"I've been here. Alason sent his Guard after me and I took off."

I study him as he refuses to make eye contact with me.

Did he not worry that I was alone? That he left me with a concern?

My thought must be loud across my face because he rushes out, "I heard of the banishment and worked out a way to get you here. Back to me where you belong."

Fixing the shreds of my dress back into place, I nod slowly. Standing up and making my way toward him.

"I missed you, Max."

Chapter 17

The door flies open and smashes against the wall. Turning quickly, I tuck myself behind Maxim.

My mouth falls open, eyes wide. Pushing Maxim away I throw myself into Hollis's arms. He catches me, spinning as he crushes me to his chest. Looking up, beaming at him, I notice he's scowling at Max.

Thumbing him on his back brings his attention back to me, a warm smile taking over his face, eyes melting with warmth.

"Scar, I've missed you. Maxim should have left you with Everett until we all got here."

His gaze returns to Maxim, glaring at him.

"You take too long to get ready, pretty boy," Max snaps back at him.

"You've been here, Hollis?"

"Yes, I was ... *sent* here after leaving the Clan."

I search his face, confusion clouding my features. A throat clears from behind us, leaning over. I see The Master's Guard standing in the doorway.

My face pales as I slowly back away from Hollis, my arms dropping to my side.

"Actually, the entire Guard has been here."

Xavier is pushed, falling to his side on the floor as a very angry Everett comes stomping in pushing past Hollis.

He reaches into his pocket, pulling out the book hidden there. His gaze lands on Maxim and swings back, punching him solidly in the face.

I watch horrified as Max falls to the floor, blood oozing from his nose.

"He's snoring," Louie says from behind me, leaning over Max's crumbled form. Everett shrugs before plopping down on the bed, laying on his belly, and flipping through his book.

I cover my mouth, attempting to keep a shocked laugh at bay.

"Why did you hit him?" I hiss through chuckles bubbling up.

Everett shrugs again, not taking his attention from his book.

Kneeling on the floor, I rest Maxim's head in my lap. Wiping the blood from his face, he snorts awake, causing the guards to laugh.

One by one, they file into the room, high-fiving Everett on their way to the opposite wall where they sit on the floor or lounge in the armchairs.

"What was that for?" Max yells, struggling to his feet.

"Because he felt like it, dumbass," Hollis replies over his shoulder before taking a seat next to Everett.

Maxim scowls, stomping off toward the bathing chamber.

I study the Guard for a moment before turning back to Hollis, a brow raised.

"We are here because we have to be. I'm your guard, my dedication is to you. They..." he motions towards the Master's Guard, "Are here because they are branded to you. In the embroidery. The Master tasked them with watching over you, they literally can't be anywhere else."

I study him closely, reaching behind myself and rubbing the tips of my fingers over the tattoo.

"Does he know they are here?"

"Yes."

"Does he know that Alason went against his word?"

"Also yes. But don't worry about him. Brenu's probably crying into a whiskey right about now," he mumbles, offhandedly before adding loudly, "You reek of sex, by the way."

My mouth drops open, ready to address why the most powerful male of all realms would be crying when Max wraps an arm around my waist, pulling me into him.

"Since we're all here and have gotten our aggression out," he glares at Everett, "Let's talk about what needs to happen next."

He settles me on the bed between Hollis and Everett, seeming to weigh his words.

"Have you really been banished?"

The room falls heavy with silence.

"Yes. The Kings and their courts have voted on it," The words vibrate through me. I refuse to acknowledge it, shoving down the pain it solicits.

"I have an idea, Lottie," he turns, pacing as he runs his hands through his hair.

"Have you noticed the wrongness within our realm? Just within this clan; the crops are dying, the water is drying up, and there isn't enough food or shelter for everyone.

"Within the Fire Clan, there is snow falling during the summer. The Air clan hasn't been able to produce hatchlings in a decade. And Water is losing their ability to swim. Their hatchlings are born without fins or gills."

His body vibrates, passion spilling from him as he describes his plight.

"Have you heard? Have you noticed?"

I shake my head, confused.

"I thought only the land was dying. What is happening to our species—I hadn't heard of it."

"That's because the Kings want to believe it is purely a realm issue. That's why Alason wants to trade you like a clawter for slaughter," he spits out, disgust clouding his face.

My heart stops. *I didn't realize it was so bad.*

"I have a solution."

Sitting down next to me, Max whispers tenderly.

"I would die of a broken heart if you were taken from me."

"What do you propose we do then? I'm banished, branded a traitor. I can't make changes. In case you forgot my miserable ascendance."

"The Master of Realms. He has a link, a key. It opens the door for mortals to be able to walk between realms."

My body tenses and it takes every ounce of strength I have not to make eye contact with those around me. *The Master's Guards. Max doesn't know.*

Max continues, oblivious to the danger he is wading into, "He doesn't need it obviously, because he controls them. If we were to take all mortals of Destrui and move them, we could use it to hold the door open for us to pass." He pauses, winding his fingers through my hair and pressing his forehead to mine.

"Will you help me? Please. I just want to do what is best for our people. Think of the hatchlings that are dying," his voice ragged, tears spilling over onto his cheeks.

My heart breaks at his plea for help.

"Surely you agree that we have to do something?" he whispers urgently.

"Like what?" I whisper back, not wanting to cause him any further distress.

"If we can take the key from The Master, we can bring everyone to a new realm, one that will grow and prosper with us in it. It'll restore our creatures."

I consider this for a moment. *It's what I've always wanted. To bring peace and prosperity to our lands. To be able to prosper for generations.*

What he is asking of me could get me killed, Goddess, it will get Max killed once the Guard reports back. Could stealing from Master Brenu be the simple solution? Can we possibly anger him and still be allowed to leave without the slaughter of our souls?

"What do you need me to do?" I finally ask.

He kisses me, hard. Fire burning along our veins.

"You have to go back to Alason. Let me handle the rest."

Chapter 18

The roars of the Guard blast out around us. Everyone arguing and rounding on Maxim.

"She will do no such thing! I've had enough of your shit, Max," Hollis is within inches of Max's face, his fangs on full display.

"Quiet." My voice should barely make a dent in the noise, but everyone around me halts.

"Before I decide to let Everett eat you, explain yourself, Maxim."

I will not willingly go back into that room. Forced into solitude, left to widdle away until my mind breaks.

Taking my hand in his, Maxim leads me to a door at the back of the chamber. Throwing it open and stopping short, I gawk. The room is filled with cauldrons and vials. Lining the shelves are more manuscripts resembling those within the Cists. Tables are pushed against the walls, bearing all manner of tools, knives, and spoons.

On the table closest to us, I spot the book Everett used to make a potion the last time we were here.

"This is a workroom," Max states, guiding me further in.

"I've never seen this part of the Cists," I pick up a handful of flowers, marveling at the brittle petals and seeds spilling out.

"It kind of... appeared. I'm not sure how we opened it," Max muses.

He holds up a small vial, showing it to the Guard.

"This is for Soul-Travel. You have to let Alason go through with the banishment ceremony. We need him to believe that you are gone from this place." his voice doesn't waver in his conviction.

Hollis backs up a step, watching Max with interest.

"Why wouldn't I be gone?"

"I'm going to send you to Gehenna–it's similar to a dream-realm. More accurate, I guess, would be calling it a different timeline.

"Nothing bad can happen to you there. You won't be harmed at all. The reason you won't be harmed is that we can't send you physically. We can't jump realms or timelines without The Master's key—but our souls can.

"You'll be here, physically. But your soul will be there. We only have enough potion for one. Now, all of us will *appear* to be there with you. But that's because we can view your experience through your thoughts; it allows us to come and go."

I nod, calming my expression.

"You can't just appear there, so we need a history for you."

I look at the Guards, their faces hard and unyielding. If I squint hard enough I can envision steam billowing out of their ears.

Swallowing thickly, I pick up the vial he's holding out to me. With shaking hands, I peer deep into the midnight blue liquid. It's thick like syrup.

"If I were to drink this, how long would I have?" I ask, betraying my calm persona.

"A day. Twenty hours at the least." Max shrugs, scratching his neck and peering around the room.

"How do you get me back here?"

"We know where they are sending you, we will be there to collect you from the Guards. I have a safe house in that area. It's where my home is."

"What's my history?"

"I can tell you, but you won't remember this conversation. Or anything that wasn't added to the potion," he shrugs, sighing before adding, "Just your life until this moment. Banished by your family, sent to live out your days as a traitor to your people. Oh, I thought it would be good for you to have a companion, someone who would be constant in your life. I've named him Nick.

"It's a good cover since it's mostly true. Everything else that happens is up to how your soul perceives its new life and provides information to you."

"You'll all be there?" I ask nervously. The guards cringe, eyes darting to each other.

It's Hollis that answers me, a warning shining in his eyes, "We will be there."

I watch as his knuckles turn white while he clenches them into fists.

"We will be there in soul, no matter what. You will never be alone."

Looking back at Maxim, I study his beautiful emerald eyes. At war with myself.

I wanted to heal this world. Plan A didn't work, so I guess it's Plan B.

"Okay. I'll do it." I tilt the potion back and swallow. The acid burns my mouth and throat, causing me to gasp and clutch my chest. Maxim grabs me, clutching me to him.

"I love you, Little Mate. Come back to me quickly."

Hollis bears his teeth at Maxim, rage pouring from him. Stepping in Hollis's path, I wrap my arms around him.

"I have to try. I love you, Hollis."

I hold out my hand to Everett, clasping his rough palm in mine.

There is a very real possibility that I won't see them again. At least not soon.

Holding back tears, I release them. Nodding to the Merry Males, I straighten my spine. Everything is moving in slow motion around me as I glance around the makeshift bedroom one more time. Walking out of the door I feel my heart crumbling, only the duty to my realm propelling my feet forward.

I'm at the door of the Cists when a finger runs along my elbow. Everett's large eyes staring back at me causes me to hesitate.

He wants to come with me.

"If something happens to me Ev, you've always been my favorite. The closest to my heart. The only one who sees me for who I am."

His chin drops to his chest. Rising it again slowly, yellow flashing through his irises, he palms my chest, pushing down hard on my heart. Tears burn his eyes while he curls his lip up determined not to cry.

I place a tender kiss on his lips before kissing the scars across his face.

The ones I put there.

Wiping away the lone tear that fought its way free, I release him. Turning back toward the door, I take a deep breath.

It's now or never.

Pushing open the door, I freeze. Even the air around me stops moving.

Alason's Guard stands before me, menacing and grinning down at me.

"Seems the traitor has tried to escape."

Everett, beneath me on the stairs, tries to push past me. Careful not to move too much, I kick toward him, my foot colliding with muscle and bone.

Crawling out slowly, I keep my eyes trained on the males in formation.

"You all alone here, female?" one grunts out at me.

Nodding my head, I swiftly close the door, pushing the sod back over it.

"Why didn't you come down to collect me if you knew I was here?" I ponder, moving swiftly away from the door. My eyes dart to it for a moment, praying that Everett doesn't come bursting through.

I've put him through so much, it's the least I can do to spare him this.

"That's a Cist, why would we bother the guardians? Do we look like we want to be cursed?"

There is a whip sounding through the air, Alason landing in his dragon only feet away from us. He runs toward me, snapping his long teeth around my forearm.

Shaking his head roughly, he pulls me to the ground under him, one paw searing my abdomen.

Letting the shift overtake him, his mortal form grins down at me, a boot holding me in the place where his paw had been.

"The Royal Courts are awaiting your procession through town. We plan on celebrating your banishment. Wouldn't want to disappoint now, would we?"

I don't resist as they collar me in chains and lead me through the forest.

Chapter 19

The bodies lining the palace walls have been preyed upon by animals. What remains of their rotting flesh peels from their bones. Limbs that have deteriorated and fallen from their host lay in the dust below them. My stomach turns, threatening to release what little it holds. Males of my Royal Court rutt against any dead body with a usable hole, deranged in their desire for release.

I try not to look, not to stare, but I find myself searching for Malinda or Oz to know if they've suffered the same horrible fate.

For their sake, I hope they have. This would be better than being enslaved to Alason's Guard.

Shackled, I'm led through the village. Commoners with hands over their hearts and heads bowed greet me. Females cry silently behind their partners. Some fall to the ground in despair before being dragged back up by those around them and dragged behind the crowds lining the street.

Please don't cry for me, you'll end up on the wall.

Separated from them, the courts of the other Royal Clans sneer and laugh as I'm dragged along behind the Guard. I refuse to cower to them, keeping my chin pointed toward the sky, my features hard.

I've accepted this fate. It's been coming since the beginning.

They lead me deep into the woods, their boots causing dry earth to descend as we march through a sandstorm. They trudge on, dragging me behind them. The Royals follow along overhead, the commoners following in our wake leaving a trail of white daisies in their stead. A tribute to a Queen supposed to save them.

Reaching the edge of our lands, the dragons in front of me halt, causing me to trip over the chains around my legs.

"Through this land is where we are meant to leave you. The Vanquish of Inbetween," a male behind me says.

I look around, there is nothing. Out ahead of me is a barren wasteland, with nothing to see or protect from the elements.

Cautiously, the male unlocks my cuffs, backing away quickly.

"We are to deliver you to the keeper of this place, but we must fly. You are to cooperate to the fullest or we rip your throat out. Understood?"

I nod, not daring to show an ounce of emotion. I shift quickly, staring at him through dead eyes. He re-attaches the manacles around my neck, tugging to make sure they are secure

We launch into the sky as one. I turn slightly, looking back over my shoulder. The commoners of our Clan packed together watching my departure, some falling to their knees as grief consumes them.

Alason leads our pack, the Royal Courts following closely. A small keep appears in the distance, a pinprick on the barren landscape. It's placed in the middle of nothing. Just dirt and dust as far as the eye can see.

Alason and the Courts veer downward, landing outside the rundown building.

I'm dragged along behind, the Guards crowding me in their mortals. I let the shift wash over me, staring diligently at Alason as I do. The Royal Courts file into the building, Lydia waving at me and grinning as she passes by.

"Come, Scarlett. Let's get started."

The Guard leads me into the building just as I hear the beat of wings. Turning my head, small turquoise dragons are heading toward us. I pull slightly at the chain around my neck, excitement rolling through me, but the Guard is already alerted. The small dragons surround us, roaring loudly.

I'm pulled toward the keep, the Guard determined to get me inside and away from them. Looking over my shoulder, a large hazel dragon catches my eye. Green eyes glowing in the twilight and headed straight for us.

The bond springs to life, tightening and pulling me toward him. Landing with a solid thud on the dirt in front of us, Maxim snorts loudly before letting out a roar that echoes across the desert.

He shifts into his mortal, taking in the males surrounding me. The small turquoise dragons inch closer to him, guarding his flank.

"Max–" I call, elation running through me. A hand is slapped over my mouth as Alason makes his way to us. His Guard splits, letting him pass.

"Maxim. You're just in time, please head in and have a seat. Bring Scarlett, everyone is waiting."

My eyes dart between Alason and Maxim, the former elated and the other grim.

Max doesn't look at me. Keeping his head low, just trudges toward the building, the dragons at his back. The Guard pushes me forward, keeping arrows pointed from all sides as we walk through the stone walls.

The heavy door opens to a long hall with four doors closed off to prying eyes. It's homey inside, humble but wealthy. They lead me to the last door at the end of the hall, open and welcoming all inside. My feet turn to stone at the threshold, rooting themselves to the floor at the sight before me.

The Royal Courts are situated in stands that ascend to the ceiling of the room. Each court separated and seated only with their Elemental Clan, their Kings situated on a single throne at the base of each grouping.

What draws my attention the most, drowning out all noise and chatter for those around me is the altar in the center of the room. An altar that Alason is standing next to smiling broadly.

The Guard pushes me, causing me to fall to my knees. They drag me forward by the chains around my ankles. The wood flooring gouges my back and arms, leaving splinters under my skin before Alason's Guard forces me upright next to Alason and Maxim.

"Your Majesties, those of the Courts," Alason's big voice booms out, quieting the room, "Thank you all for joining me in our quest to heal our realm."

Applause breaks out, deafening.

Raising his hands, Alason continues. "We have agreed that banishment was a fair trial for the commoners to accept, but the most beneficial and just punishment for treason and illegal magic would be sacrificial in nature. All those in favor say, 'Aye.'"

The room erupts. Those jumping to their feet and cheering appear soundless and colorless to me.

"Scarlett of Earth, Daughter of King Vika and Consort Tilla, mate to Maxim of the Inbetween, you have been sentenced to death. Sacrificed to the God of Aether to grant favor for our lives. The fates have seen it and all will be restored, as it once was. Consider this an honor to serve your world."

Maxim is staring at the floor, ignoring the tears pouring down my face as I stare hate into him.

You lied to me! You knew this would happen!

I attempt to send my contempt down the bond to him. Instead, images of Everett and Hollis invade me.

I'll never see them again.

My vision is fading, my body struggling to keep me upright.

I must stay strong, I will not let them break me.

Hands of the Guard wrap around my arms and legs forcibly hoisting me onto the altar of white marble. There is a bed of flowers awaiting me there. Pure white daisies lay on a bed of white satin trimmed in gold.

"You like them?" Alason mumbles, "Maxim picked them all himself."

My sight tunnels until the only thing I can focus on is the somber face of the male I love. A loud pop snaps inside of me, the bond breaking into dust. The pain radiates through me as though Max's betrayal wields a whip, slicing me apart from the inside out.

My knees crumple beneath me, unable to support me any longer. Alason wraps an arm around my waist, holding my sagging body up against him.

"Dragons of Destrui, give thanks to your savior as we end her life to begin our own."

With his final words, he pushes me toward Maxim. Placing an arm behind my neck and the other under my knees, he carefully lies me on the berth of flowers.

They mock me, their symbol of purity and innocence laid out as an offering for a God that won't serve them. I hope it's worth it.

My eyes slowly fall shut, like I've been awake for days and my body can't fight sleep any longer.

The Soul-Travel...

Max's eyes vanish before appearing before me again, getting further away every time, before disappearing altogether.

"I'm sorry, Little Mate."

Chapter 20

My eyes fly open at the endearment, just in time to see Alason wielding a dagger aimed straight at my heart. It sinks in, blood slowly oozing out around it. He gives it a final twist before leading the courts in prayer to Aether. One by one, the Clans approach, laying a variety of white flowers over my body. I close my eyes, begging to die already and be taken from this horror.

The room empties slowly, the celebration fading as they exit the hall. Sitting up, I climb off the bed and stand from the altar, watching as Maxim falls to his knees beside my tomb.

"It didn't work."

He doesn't acknowledge me, doesn't even look over to where I'm standing.

The door swings wide, shaking in its frame before cracking and falling to the ground below.

"I've been saying for days that I could kill you. It appears I finally have an actual reason to," Hollis snarls, picking up Maxim by his collar and squeezing his long fingers around Max's throat.

The Merry Males filter in behind him, setting up a perimeter around the altar.

"She's... not... dead," Max chokes out, digging his nails into Hollis's hand.

Well, obviously. My face pales at his words, I try again.

"Excuse me, but obviously it didn't work."

Hollis throws Maxim to the ground, stomping toward the altar and peeking inside the tomb. I follow him, looking over his shoulder.

My body is still lying there as though I'm sleeping.

Or dead if you consider the blade sticking out of my chest and the blood drying around it.

Connected to my chest is a thin thread leading from my body to this being I now am.

It's my soul, my lifestrings keeping me tethered to this realm. No wonder they can't hear or see me.

Climbing into the tomb, Hollis cradles my limp form to him, brushing my hair back from my face. He places his lips on my hair, closes his eyes, and rocks my body back and forth, tears slipping down his cheeks.

"She took the potion, she's fine," Maxim croaks out, picking himself up from the floor.

"You didn't tell her the truth about *that* either," Hollis whispers, still rocking my body back and forth.

"Her soul has to decide how her life plays out, I can't control everything," Max whispers back.

"That realm will not keep her safe!" Abel snarls from his corner, "When Brenu finds her there, he will be furious. It's a land of torture. No one just comes and goes from there unscathed."

"You could have told her," Max sniffs.

"We can not interfere with her free will, asshole. But you already knew that, didn't you?"

The Merry Males move as one, advancing on Max and yelling at him, fangs and claws at the ready.

Movement to my left catches my attention. Everett is painting a mural on the wall at the head of the altar. Walking to him, I attempt to run my fingers along the black scarred flesh covering his face.

"He let you have her on the agreement that you and the Guard would keep Scarlett from harm. We can't protect her from her fate, but we can try to protect her from you," Hollis snarls, laying my body down carefully before striding across the room and stabbing Max in the chest with his finger.

My soul is being pulled high toward the ceiling as though I'm floating while I watch this unfold. Those around me seem to blur around the edges, musing together to form a blob in my vision.

Who allowed Max to keep me? Alason?

Everett turns, flipping off Max in the process. Leaning over my body, he tenderly places a kiss on my hair, nuzzling his face against mine. Then one by one, the Master's Guard disappears into the mural.

I thought no one could jump realms without the Master's key.

Read on for a sneak peek of:

MURALS AND SOULS

Murals and Souls

The rain is falling against the glass, causing the world outside to look even bleaker than normal. Taking a deep breath, I step away and frown at the room surrounding me.

"Scarlett, why don't you come explore the rest of the house? It'll do you some good to become familiar with it."

I turn to look at Nicholas standing in the doorway, forcing a smile for his benefit.

"Oh, I was just going to unpack in here first. Make sure everything is squared away for when we sleep tonight. Don't you agree?"

I'm trying hard to be optimistic for his benefit, but I think he can see right through me. Diverting my attention to the room, my brow furrows. A pair of arms wrap around me and Nicholas mutters into the top of my hair,

"Looks like you've finished everything." *I don't remember unpacking this.* The room is furnished in dark colors: black, red, and gray. Even the wooden floors beneath my feet are dark brown.

Grinning, I tease Nicholas, "At least you let me pick out the decor. This screams 'happily-married male.'"

He laughs out loud at me, throwing his head back and spins me around in his arms so that I'm pressed to his chest.

"Ah, but a happily married male I am, Mrs. Somnium."

Dragons of Destrui
Series Order:

1. Daggers and Daisies
2. Murals and Souls - January 2023 (Preorder Now)
3. Vengeance and Violence - To be announced
4. Gods and Dragons - To be announced

Thank You

Thank you so much for taking a chance on Daggers and Daisies. I hope you love this backward realm as much as I do. When I say love, I mean hate. Their laws are terrible, aren't they?

Want to know what happens to Scarlett next? Murals and Souls is the second book in the Dragons of Destrui Series that will leave you an emotional mess. Tear-stained, heartbroken, with a spark of happily-ever-after that keeps you hanging on and second-guessing until the very end. You'll be begging for more.

I would love for you to join my reader group, Arlin Creed, so we can connect and share thoughts on Daggers and Daisies and all of the wonderful things happening within the Destrui Series. The Facebook group is the first place to find out about new releases, cover reveals, book news, and connect with others who enjoy this series as much as you!

About the Author:

Arlin Creed cultivated her passion for writing as a young girl in Southeast Louisiana where books were an escape from the tragedy of Earth into extraordinary realms where life was always beautiful. She believed stories in all forms and genres could open portals to the imagination and heal weary souls. Arlin Creed is a published fantasy novelist whose books include The Dragons of Destrui Series, despite her high school ELA teacher giving her a "D" on all creative writing assignments. She is currently working on the third in the series.

Please visit the Arlin Creed official social media pages to read excerpts, reviews, and view book trailers.

Facebook: ArlinCreed
Instagram:@author_arlincreed
Twitter:@arlincreed

Acknowledgments

This has been a journey one could write about, a tale of a heroine born into tragedy and soul-crushing trauma then led into the light and healed by those around her. My grandmother often compares my life to the movie *Homeless to Harvard.* I always laugh and thank her when she says that, not realizing just how true those words are.

To my precious readers and to those who started with nothing- don't give up. Your grand adventure is awaiting you. You are almost to your goal, even if your goal is as simple as mine was: To live in a house made of bricks with three bedrooms, a/c in the summer, and heat in the winter with a steady job and paycheck to buy food.

I didn't realize how much putting words on paper and "throwing myself to the wolves" would do for me. Saying these novels were a labor of love is an understatement.

Thank you to my husband. Taylor without you this would have never happened. You challenged me, by uttering those magic words that I "wouldn't" do something, you brought out the brat in me and I was determined to prove you wrong. You said I wouldn't write one book, so I wrote four just to prove my point. You unknowingly forced me to face my fears of rejection and criticism and, in doing so, led me to discover something I love.

Thank you to my mother-in-law, who cried happy tears right along with me when I received my first printed copy. You hugged me and told me you were so proud of me, that you always knew I would be good at writing because I have such an imagination. Thank you for being the most amazing mom to me, I don't know what I did in a past life to deserve you.

Thank you to my best friend, my soul's person. Shire you are the world's best cheerleader. From page one, you've always been honest and upfront and I can't thank you enough for that. Especially when you told me, "I was afraid your books were going to suck. And I would have to tell you because I'm not going to let you go out there and embarrass both of us." You got me through every plot hole, every conviction that the series was a dumpster fire, and through every weekly conversation where I was convinced I was a fraud.

Thank you Whitney for editing and offering suggestions and comments throughout the entire process, and for being patient with me when I made change after change to the manuscript. Thank you for giving music to my stories that evoked emotions, provided drive and focus while I was writing. You helped bring Scarlett to life. She would be a shell without you.

And finally, to my readers. That target audience every writer craves. My 'Resa. My very first ever reader. Thank you for reading the hot-mess express, unedited, grammar-ruined manuscripts. That must have killed your ELA teacher's heart. But you cheered me on and hosted private book club where we could drink and discuss. Your pride in me is infectious, proclaiming "amazing" and daring anyone to say otherwise. I don't know what I would do without you. One day, when I'm rich and famous, I'll retire you and you can be drunk every day.

Haili, you are fantastic and gave me so much guidance and honest, true feedback and provided my very first glowing review. Also, thank you for understanding the deep love a parent has for Bluey.

CPSIA information can be obtained
at www.ICGtesting.com
Printed in the USA
LVHW110434121022
730468LV00005B/205

9 798218 078089